THE DARK GLANCER

Andrew Lee

David,
Glancer is always
the answer

David

Eleanor is always

she answer me

DEDICATION

To JLS, who made me pull this book out of the trash multiple times to bring it back to life and ultimately finish.

ACKNOWLEDGMENTS

This book was written between December of 2020 to February of 2023. Thanks to all those who helped and encouraged me along the way. And to those of you who bought the t-shirt up front as well. Jenny, Jeff, Garo, Bonnie, Ally, Ivan, David, Kori, Andrew, Jacque, Mike C. I don't know if I will ever try this again but it was a fun ride.

CONTENTS

CHAPTER 1

$2 GLANCER NIGHT

It's a Wednesday. The time is around 9 p.m. in Glancerville East, a rough part of the city of Glancerville. Years ago, this was a prominent part of the city, but today it's mostly seedy bars and one amazing strip club.

Dwayne has lived here for the last 15 years. A few were good, but many more hard. For a laughingstock like Dwayne, those tough times feel endless.

Dwayne has had a long day, and as usual, he is about to decompress and blow off steam at his usual spot, the Landing Strip Bar and Grille. The Landing Strip has been a staple of the East for decades. His family has a long history there, and Dwayne has established quite the legacy of his own, but not quite in the same way.

The Landing Strip is the kind of place where patrons better know how to use their fists, where people religiously avoid flushing the toilet or washing their hands. The Landing Strip is famous for two things: the quick-witted, sarcastic Marie, who has been bartending there six nights a week for the past 17 years; and the much-beloved Glancer beer, whose slogan, "Glancer is Always the Answer," is plastered all around the city.

Glancer beer has a long tradition in Glancerville. It was named after the town's founder, the legendary Conrad Glancer, who opened the Landing Strip years before he invented his fine pilsner, distributed it nationally and started raking in millions. Glancer beer has a great taste and smooth delivery, and no one loves it—or the Landing Strip—more than Dwayne.

Glancer beer has grown into the cornerstone of the economy and is the pride of the town. Many, many years earlier, Conrad Glancer invented it, and it quickly became a commercial success nationwide. The town eventually renamed itself after the beer and the man in the 1940's. The Glancer Brewing Company was the number one employer in the city. Conrad had grown it from a one-man operation out the back door of the Landing Strip to eventually becoming the economic juggernaut of an entire city. Conrad was a legend in Glancerville. He invented the beer when he was just 24 years old. It did not take him much past his early 30s to establish himself as the richest man in Glancerville. He made millions selling his beer out of the Landing Strip, and in the early 1930s, he opened up his very own mass production plant in what would become downtown Glancerville and took his product national.

However, the man himself was far from perfect. A known womanizer, Conrad had three children—all boys and all from different women. In the 1960s, he introduced Glancer Dark. The public felt the name was unwelcoming, and it never saw the light of day. Conrad was heartbroken, and many believed the failure of his new product put him in an early grave. Many years later, his grandson, Conrad Glancer III vowed to re-establish Glancer Dark as dark beers were now a staple in society at long last.

Dwayne can be found at the Landing Strip almost every night. It is truly his home away from home. On this Wednesday night in September, Dwayne is sitting in his usual spot at the bar, staring aimlessly at the television and contemplating why his life has never rebounded from that fateful night 20 years ago. In other words, it was a typical day of the week in the life of Dwayne St. Thomas. A life which has put him on the map, but a map nobody would want to be on.

"So, would you like another beer or are you calling it a night?" Marie asks.

Dwayne looks up at his favorite bartender. "Don't ask dumb questions to dumb people," he says. "Bring on the next victim, the next Glancer."

Marie shakes her head in amusement and sympathy. "I'll make it a bucket, Stain," she says, using a common nickname for Dwayne. "How about that?"

"Sounds good to me."

Marie fills up a bucket with five Glancers and brings it over to Dwayne. Over the next several hours, he drinks beer after beer while patrons come and go. By the fourth beer, he starts to tilt in and out of sleep, a common thing for him after too many Glancers.

Marie notices. "Maybe you have had enough, Dwayne."

Dwayne looks up at Marie in embarrassment and agrees. "Yeah, probably. So, babe, how about the check?"

Marie walks to the cash register and works on ringing Dwayne up. Just then, the front door of the bar opens, and in walks a charming couple, Rick and Hildy. Rick and Hildy have a long, dark history with Dwayne. They spot him and immediately begin their usual antics of giving him a hard time and bullying him.

"Hey Marie, better get Dr. Poo an Uber. Looks like he is in the bag again," laughs Rick.

Marie does not find it amusing. "Mind your business, Rick. You are such an asshole. Stain hasn't done anything to you."

Marie then pours a glass of water on sleepy Dwayne's head and hands him the check.

"Christmas Night! Marie, it's $30. What the hell? I thought it was $2 Glancer night?"

"Um, yeah, it is!! You had 16 Glancers. I took care of the last one for you, babe, since you're a regular."

"This is horseshit Marie." Still, Dwayne hands over his debit card and tips his usual 12 percent. Marie does not mind, she knows the daily struggle Dwayne goes through.

Rick notices an inebriated Dwayne struggling to get up. "Don't forget to put your wallet in your pocket, Stain."

"Yeah," adds Hildy, "you wouldn't want anything to slip out." Hildy and Rick both laugh hysterically in Dwayne's direction.

"You two are such assholes to Dwayne. He's never done anything to hurt you. You're bullies," says Marie, defending her loyal customer and friend.

Dwayne gets up from the bar, walks toward Rick, and looks him square in the eyes.

"Someday, I don't know how and I don't know when, but you are going to pay for ruining my life, Rick Townsend. If I ever have my way, you will pay, but I just don't…"

Rick cuts Dwayne off. "Go get a shave. By the way, Stain, if 'ifs" and 'buts' were beers and sluts, oh what a party we would have. Come on, Hildy, let's go play some pool. Time for Stain to get his Uber."

"Or maybe his pooper," laughs Hildy.

"Classic babe, classic."

Dwayne, unfazed, stumbles out the door into the parking lot. He lights up a Doral, his cigarette of choice.

"$3 a pack and worth every cent," he says to himself.

His Uber pulls up.

"I'm looking for Dwayne," asks the driver.

"That's me."

He gets in the Uber after crushing his cigarette onto the ground. The driver takes off, occasionally glancing at Dwayne in the rearview mirror.

"Man, you look familiar," he says after a few minutes. "Do I know you? Are you famous? I know that face. Did we go to the same high school dance 20 years ago? You know, the famous one?"

"You don't know me, friend. Just drive and keep the chatter to a minimum," Dwayne fires back.

Another six blocks pass by until the car reaches Lowman Road and Dwayne's apartment complex, Lost Soul Lofts. Across the street, the neon lights of the Tainted Horse Strip Club shine bright. A scrappy dive where the locals go. Dwayne frowns at his empty wallet.

"Not tonight, ladies," he says. He blows them a kiss and heads home.

CHAPTER 2

PITTFALLS OF LIFE

After a late night, Dwayne lies asleep in his clothes from the night before with the television on in the background and drool coming down his face.

Dwayne lives in the infamous Lost Souls Lofts in Glancerville East. It is a 200-unit cookie cutter complex known for its proximity to the Tainted Horse and its low water pressure. Dwayne has a 350-square-feet unit, which not a lady has ever visited. It is decorated with Doral cigarette empty packs and an array of empty Glancer bottles. Outside there is a hot tub, rarely cleaned, in which several young ladies from the Tainted Horse have dipped their toes in during the wee hours of the morning.

The Lost Souls Apartments is not a complex where anybody in their right mind strives to live. It is a place where people wind up. People like Dwayne and his best friend, Larry.

On his nightstand is an alarm clock and a half empty beer bottle. As Dwayne slumbers, his alarm clock begins to sound, and after several minutes of fighting with the snooze button, he awakens, sits up and grabs the bottle on his nightstand. He finishes it with one big pull. He then lets out a belch and focuses his attention on the television news.

Dwayne only watches the local news, mostly for the morning anchors, Greg and Jane. He sleeps with the television on just so he can awaken to the sounds of their voices. Greg and Jane are like another addiction to Dwayne. He often hates them, but he can't stop watching.

"Glancerville is expected to beef up security in the Downtown District as the city expects record crowds two weeks from tomorrow night as it marks the famous White Pants Festival. The festival, in which thousands flock the city streets for a night of fashion, drinks, art, and of course, cocaine," reports Jane.

"You know Jane, September 25 also marks the twenty-year anniversary of the Dwayne St. Thomas incident," says Greg."

"Oh my God, who can forget that? What a disaster!"

"Yeah, Jane, it really made the sophomore dance at Glancervill High a thing of legends. The song 'Free Bird' has never been the same to me. Also, don't forget, Jane, local rock legends Dirty Urine are headlining this year's festival. I just love their debut hit from years ago, 'My Stream is Your Dream,'" adds Greg.

"Their entire debut album, UTI, was classic, absolutely classic."

Dwayne is in disbelief. "Really! You have nothing better to talk about?"

He throws his empty beer bottle at the television set, begins to take his clothes off, and starts the shower.

"Stupid White Pants Festival," he mumbles to himself.

Just then, the television switches over to commercials. It features Dwayne's nemesis sitting in a hot tub. The commercial begins.

"Hi, I'm Rick Townsend, local legend and COO of Glancerville's feature event, White Pants Festival. There is nothing I enjoy more than a cold beer from Glancer. Glancer is the leader in taste, we all know that. For over 85 years, we have been enjoying the fine pilsner created by Conrad Glancer right here in our very own Glancerville. Now, the Glancer family has done it again. You want more taste? Introducing Glancer Dark. It's like the great beer you love, but with a darker color and bolder taste. Hell, you could probably drink this at work, and your boss would think it was a soda pop." At this, Rick laughs and points at the camera. "Just don't let him smell your breath," he continues. "Remember folks, when in doubt, Glancer is always the answer!"

As the commercial comes to an end, Dwayne is not at all impressed. "Dark beer? Gross! I'll stick to my fine regular Glancer pilsner."

Dwayne gets in the shower. He needs to be at work in 30 minutes. He hates his job, and really, who could blame him? He's working at the school where his life was forever changed.

Dwayne emerges from the shower and walks into the bedroom, where he methodically puts on a gray janitor's suit. He then puts on his dingy sneakers and reaches for his name tag. He stares long and hard at it and frowns: Dwayne St. Thomas. The name is a heavy burden to carry.

He walks out of his front door and is immediately met by his neighbor and longtime best friend Larry in the corridor.

"Hey, Dwayne, off to work?"

Dwayne is in no mood for banter.

"Take a hike, Larry."

Larry is amused. Dwayne's daily bad attitude is nothing new to him. He understands the history and why his friend is this way. "See you at happy hour, Stain."

"I'll be there. Have a cold Glancer waiting for me. Tell Marie! Don't shortchange me on my bar tab, dammit. She charged me $30 for 16 Glancers last night."

Larry shakes his head as he looks at Dwayne.

"That cheap whore! I'll tell her DST, a cold one will be waiting for you upon your arrival. Have a good day at work."

Dwayne walks out the door, gets in his Chevy Spark and leaves for work.

Dwayne is very proud of his car. "She has 115,000 miles and is still going strong. Road precision at its finest, the Spark," he says to himself.

He lights a cigarette as he pulls out of the parking lot. He pops a cassette into the tape deck. As Dirty Urine's greatest hits play, he begins thinking about the night before, about Rick and Hildy and how badly he wants revenge.

But before long, his thoughts turn to the long day facing him. There's work, then a doctor's appointment, and finally a rendezvous with Larry at the Landing Strip.

A full day, he thinks.

Minutes later, Dwayne pulls up in the parking lot of Glancer Valley High School. He gets out of the Spark and stares at the school.

"Well, shit," he mumbles to himself. "Another day in paradise."

Dwayne has been working at Glancerville High School as the head janitor for several years. It is not a glamorous or well-paying gig, but a man with his history can't be choosy. He's lucky to even have a job in this town. Principal Pitts hired Dwayne several years later because she figured it would be good to have someone on staff as an example of what not to become in life. Dwayne has only himself to blame. His situation is self-inflicted. On one hand, the incident of 20 years ago defined his life to the worst degree, and any normal person would try to run as far away from it as they could. Yet, Dwayne, despite always feeling so full of regret, seems to oddly embrace fame when it suits him, such as in the case of his janitorial job.

Dwayne clocks in and begins his normal activities. Cleaning piss-soaked toilets, scraping gum and boogers and who knows what else from underneath desks and cafeteria tables. Mopping hallways that will be scuffed beyond recognition by the end of the day.

As he works, he can feel the judgment, scorn and pity from the kids. It's constant and uncomfortable, like a ray of blazing sunlight he can't avoid.

Students know all about Dwayne and his legacy at the school, and although only 15, 16, or 17 years old, their parents see the school yearbook and know exactly who they are looking at when the photo of janitor Dwayne St. Thomas appears in the yearly annual. The infamous events of September 25 still live on in dinner conversations around Glancerville. Sometimes the story is told to get a laugh or shock a newcomer. But mostly, it's a cautionary tale.

While he mops the hallway, a student walks by him and says, "Hey Dwayne, my main dookie stain, how are you today?"

Dwayne stops mopping and gives an evil stare. "Watch it, kid!"

Just then, a senior named Michelle walks by and says, "Hey, Dr. Poo, how's your day going?"

And so it goes on all day, every day. Just another day at the office.

Dwayne continues to mop the floor, and Principal Pitts walks over to him. There's no love lost between the two. Pitts has always been a major nemesis, never letting Dwayne forget his lowest moment. Today, she approaches him with a confident yet arrogant swagger. As if she knows she owns him, or at least his reputation.

"Hello, Dwayne," she says. "I'm going to need you to hang these posters for me today. Please put one in the library, two in the cafeteria, and three in the hallway. They're for the upcoming sophomore dance. I think you know the one."

She hands Dwayne the posters and walks away. He stares at her back as she walks away and thinks of how awful she's been to him. He asks himself again why, after all the embarrassment, he even works for this school or for her.

Dwayne begins hanging the posters in the hallway. As he hangs the posters, he recollects the time 20 years ago when he attended the same dance. The night when a simple high school social event changed his life forever. A night in which he thought he was becoming a man, but wound up a forever fractured, wounded boy. It was a night in which legends were made, and Dwayne St. Thomas certainly became a legend. However, being a legend is not always a good thing. Just then another student walked by.

"Hi Mr. Stain. Those posters must bring back some real memories. That dance was legendary, my dad says."

"Beat it, kid."

Dwayne drops the posters and hammer and lights another smoke in the middle of the high school corridor. As he inhales, he stares at the poster. "Why did I agree to go to that dance? And for the love of God, why did I wear white shorts?"

CHAPTER 3

GROSS ENCOUNTERS

At 2 p.m. on the dot, like a murmuration of starlings, a cluster of students rush out of Glancer Valley High. The excitement about leaving is evident in every one of their smiles. As he threads his way through the crush of kids, Dwayne's face is expressionless. The skies are gloomy. Rain is on its way. It's perfect weather for a visit to a psychiatrist.

Dwayne has been seeing Dr. Nelson Gross off and on for nearly 17 years. His parents gifted him weekly sessions for life when he agreed to finally move out of their house. But he only goes every couple of months. Like most things in his life, Dwayne approaches his therapy with a lack of focus and little regard.

But it's not like therapy has helped him feel any better. However, with the 20th anniversary of the incident quickly approaching, the need for Dwayne to talk about his feelings is greater than usual. He pulls into the parking lot and exits the Spark. He lights up a smoke and ponders what the next several days leading up to the anniversary will be like for him and whether he will ever be able to get over the event. Why do people still talk about it, why is it so legendary, and why did it happen to him? All such questions have been burning in the mind of Dwayne St. Thomas over the last 20 years. Dwayne crushes out the Doral and makes his way into the building, where he is met by the receptionist of Dr. Gross.

"Well, good afternoon, sir. How can I help you?" she says.

"Good afternoon! I am Dwayne St. Thomas, and I have an appointment with Dr. Gross for a therapy session. Is he available right now?"

"Have a seat, sir, he is running a few minutes late. He'll be right with you," she says. "And congratulations on the 20th anniversary!"

Dwayne has a seat in the waiting room and begins to read a random magazine silently just to kill time. He hears the receptionist on the phone with what he assumes is one of her friends.

"Yes, he is really here; he has an appointment."

There is a silent pause as she listens to the person on the other end of the receiver.

"Well, no, his pants seem fine. I think it was just a thing 20 years ago."

Dwayne stands up and decides to ask her what the hell she is talking about, but before he can, Dr. Gross emerges and puts his hand forward to Dwayne for a handshake.

"Well, hello there, Dwayne. Nice to see you. Why don't you come right in and have a seat."

"Hi Doc, good to see you as well."

Dwayne enters Dr. Gross's office and has a seat on the sofa.

Throughout the years, whenever Dwayne attended an appointment with Dr. Gross, they usually discussed his career, his personal relationships, his bad habits, and his overall station in life. Dwayne was always reluctant to get into intricate details of the incident, but today, Dwayne resolved, would be different.

"How are we doing today, Dwayne?" began Dr. Gross.

Dwayne lights up a smoke and begins to speak.

"I dunno, Doc. Just when I think things are getting better, the 20th anniversary of the incident is upon us, and people are bringing it up right and left. I just don't know how much more of this I can take. I think no matter how much I try to get over it, people will never stop reminding me about it again and again."

"That surprises me," replies Dr. Gross.

"What, that people are talking about the incident?"

"No, it surprises me that you thought things were getting better for you, Dwayne. I don't witness anything getting better at all. In fact, I think the trajectory of your personal and professional life has been in a permanent downtrend," he continued as he handed Dwayne an ashtray.

"Sorry, what do you mean, Doc?"

"Let's take a step back. Tell me about your current relationship with your family, Dwayne."

Dwayne's past is a complicated one. He was the second son of Drs. James and Jennifer St. Thomas. James was a heart surgeon, and Jennifer was a radiologist. They raised their children in the nicest part of Glancerville, and Dwayne and his oldest brother Dwight wanted for nothing.

They were well traveled, well clothed, and pillars of the community.

James and Jennifer had high expectations for their children, and Dwight did not disappoint. He graduated from Glancer High six years earlier than Dwayne, where he was a star in baseball, football, and track. He was so good, the school retired his number when he graduated and erected a statue in his honor. And he received scholarships to Glancer University in all three sports.

But it wasn't just sports. Dwight was good at everything else: school, ladies, you name it. After college, he turned down offers from the NFL and Major League Baseball and went to law school and medical school—at the same time. He currently practices medicine in the Winter and Fall and law in the Spring and Summer. Oh, and he has four perfect children, two boys and two girls.

Things were different with Dwayne, especially after "the incident." His parents supported him through high school, allowing him to sleep in the garage. Upon graduating from high school, they gave him $1,500 and lifetime therapy sessions with Dr. Gross – in exchange for him leaving the house. They occasionally write him letters and send him a little cash, but that's about it.

Dwight hasn't spoken to Dwayne in the last 18 years. Dwayne's mishap on September 25, 2001, was the singular undoing of the St. Thomas family. Sightings of James, Jennifer and Dwight in Glancerville are few and far between. They have left their city behind for Dwayne to inhabit.

"Not much still, Doc, really. No communication," answered Dwayne. "Every once in a while, I get a card with a

$100 bill from my mom or some stupid Christmas card from my brother's wife telling me all the dumb things his kids have accomplished over the past years. All four of his kids now seem like peckers to me."

"Dwayne, you ruined their lives. You can't really blame them," continued Dr. Gross.

"Hey, I was the victim," snapped Dwayne.

"No, Dwayne. Hildy was the victim. You really ruined a lot of lives."

"This is horseshit! How much are you charging for this crap? I came here all the way from Glancer Valley High just to try to feel better about myself and my situation and get some insight. You are making me feel even worse. I am sure I would have more luck drinking Glancers than talking to you."

"Dwayne, you have alluded to this episode for many sessions, but for me to really help you, I think you need to walk me through the events of the evening in question. This is really important. Remember, Dwayne, I am all ears, and take as many breaks as you need."

Dwayne thought long and hard before he spoke. He had tried as hard as he could to mentally block out that night. But could he? Whether at school, the bar, or at the psychiatrist's reception desk, he was constantly reminded of the same thing.

After a long hesitation pause, Dwayne eventually began to speak.

"Well, Doctor, it kind of went like this...."

CHAPTER 4
THE DROPPER

***

The year is 2001, and it seems things are moving right along for Dwayne. Like every other kid his age, he listens to loud music, skateboards, sneaks cigarettes in the backyard, wakes his neighbors up at night by practicing his electric guitar, and tries to get his hands on a nudie mag whenever he gets a chance. He isn't very experienced when it comes to the ways of the ladies, but that had not prevented him from making a fool of himself around them. Despite his best attempts, though, he has never been on a real date or danced with a girl, let alone gotten any real action. And so, it was expected that when Glancerville High School announced the Sophomore Dance, Dwayne was not very excited, to say the least. He knew what was coming. All the cool kids would welcome it as the athletes and cheerleaders would dance, grope each other and just have a wild time. Meanwhile, the not-so-popular kids would be peer pressured into attending and have an awkward time.

It did not help that the only girl Dwayne had any real interest in was Hildy MacMuphyn. *Boy, was she a total diva,* he thought. She was captain of the cheerleading team and dated most of the offense of the junior varsity football team. Hildy came from money and made sure everyone knew it. She wore the most expensive clothes, took her friends to the finest restaurants, and always had her chauffeur drop her at school every morning. It was only the finer things in life for her. Her mom was a socialite, and her dad was a businessman, as she told people. But everyone knew the real story—he was a prominent cocaine dealer. Hildy would go on to date Dwayne's nemesis, Rick, through her final years of high school and college, but, in 2001, she was, surprisingly, available

Larry Dugan was Dwayne's oldest friend. They had been best of buddies since 1st grade. Like Dwayne, Larry was a total loser when it came to girls and dating. They often shared their dreams of finding Miss Right and what the future would and should hold for a couple of studs like them. "Lare-Bear," as Dwayne sometimes referred to him, did not come from as ritzy a background as Dwayne, but he always had a positive attitude and was loyal to the bitter end. Larry was the one who convinced Dwayne to go to the dance.

"Hildy will be there, man. You can ask her to dance with you. It'll be fun," Larry says.

Dwayne is not convinced. "It's football season, Larry. She's spoken for."

"Nonsense Dwayne! Imagine she's the center of your team and is snapping you the ball."

"Interesting visual, Larry."

"Think about it, Dwayne. It would be worth it, trust me."

"I'll think about it," Dwayne promises.

Eventually, he comes around to the idea of going to the dance. Every other high schooler is going to be there. And no matter what, it's sure as hell going to be awkward. Why not go? Even his brother Dwight encourages him to attend, and as an incentive, he lets Dwayne borrow his favorite white shorts.

"Better return them clean, dickhead," Dwight warns as he hands over the gleaming shorts.

To celebrate, Dwayne's mom buys him a crisp blue polo shirt and brand-new white loafers. "I am so excited for you to attend your first dance," she says, the emotion catching in her voice. "I remember when Dwight went to the Sophomore Dance six years ago. He had just bought those white shorts. I remember him coming home with lipstick all over his neck and face,—and different colors at that!"

Dwayne winces. He doesn't like hearing about his brother's hookups, especially from his mom and especially when his own track record was, well, less established.

But nothing, not even his mom, can stop the excitement from building in Dwayne. By the time the dance arrived, on September 25, 2001, he's more than ready to make his big move on Hildy.

The doors to the high school gym open at 6:30 on the dot, and by 8 p.m., the place is really hopping. The DJ cranks out one power ballad after the other. Dwayne stands in the corner by himself, looking at the dancing crowd and smoking a Doral, when Larry spots him.

"Hey man, why are you standing here all by yourself? Go ask Hildy to dance with you. You have been in love with her since kindergarten, and here's your chance. Go do it!"

"Nah, man. She's out of my league. Anyway, I think she has the hots for the scumbag Rick from the football team. I used to like that guy, but he changed into one big jerk once he hit puberty. He's a total bully now. Girls like bad boys. They don't dance with guys like me."

"You have no confidence, bro, but I know what will help. Have you ever had a beer, Dwayne?"

"Gross! Don't you have to be like 21 or something? I'm just fine with my Capri Sun, Larry."

Larry was not taking no for an answer.

"Come with me to the parking lot, DST. Just trust me."

Dwayne reluctantly agrees, and they walk through the parking lot to Larry's bike. Larry unzips the backpack slung over the handlebars. Inside, Dwayne sees the glint of a six-pack of Glancer beer. Despite being raised by parents who enjoyed a nightly beer or two, Dwayne has never had a beer before.

Larry sees the concerned look on his friend's face and pleads, "Split this six-pack with me. It'll make us men. It's called Glancer. My dad said panties will drop after you have like 20 of them. But I only had the money for a six pack."

Dwayne stares at the frosty beverages, frowns, and lights another cigarette.

"I don't know, Larry. If I get caught with beer on my breath, there goes my Nintendo privileges, and Super Mario 8 is coming out next week."

"Oh, quit being a loser, Dwayne. Tonight, we ride as men!"

Dwayne hesitates, puts out his smoke, and lights another.

"Well?" Larry asks.

"Fine, what's the worst thing that can happen?"

Larry and Dwayne crack open the beers and guzzle the first two as 'Bacteria, Not My Fault' by Dirty Urine plays on Larry's boombox. Before long, a group of kids, led by Rick Townsend, approach. Rick drags a huge blue Igloo cooler behind him.

"Hey, look, it's Dork and his sidekick, Dorkster. What are you losers doing here?" Rick says with a sneer.

Not amused, Larry throws his bottle down and points right at Rick.

"Drinking Glancer beer. You should try it sometime, Rick."

"What is drinking beer going to do for losers like you?"

"Blow me, Rick. Dwayne here is going to ask Hildy to dance with him after he finishes his third Glancer."

Rick laughs out loud.

"Blow you, Larry, ha, small meal, and Hildy MacMuphyn. There is no damn way she will dance with a loser like St. Thomas."

Larry comes back, "Nobody can turn down a man who is three beers deep, Rick. Just watch."

"Ok, ok, we're all men," says Rick. "I hope she does say yes and dances with you, Dwayne. Maybe you can even get her to grab your 'Johnson.'" Rick laughs and the other guys chuckle.

Dwayne reacts, "Screw you, Rick! She may be grabbing my Johnson and Johnson."

"What does that even mean? I'll tell you what, Dwayne, I want you to dance with Hildy so bad I will give you a fourth beer, one of my own Glancers. It's straight from my dad's collection. He keeps it in his man cave so my mom won't find it. Nooch!"

Rick opens up the cooler. Dwayne scans it quickly. There are at least 40 Glancers in there, he thinks. Rick grabs a beer, opens it up, and without anyone noticing, puts a couple of eye drops into the beer. He hands the beer to Dwayne and grabs one for himself.

"Cheers, Dwayne. Drink this one with me and go get your girl."

They proceed to pound the beer. Feelings of euphoria come over Dwayne as he finishes his fourth beer. He lights another smoke.

"It's time, Lare-bear. I'm gonna get my girl."

"Ok, Dwayne, it's time. Go do this, and God speed."

He hesitates for a moment, "Ummm...I don't know, Larry...what if she says no?"

"No, she won't, Dwayne. You have had four beers. You are a man now! Quit being such a wimp. Go ask her to dance, and maybe you will even end up with some action tonight, bro. You got this, DST. I believe in you!"

"Yeah, I can do it. Totally!"

Dwayne takes a deep breath.

"Ok, remember, it's now or never!"

They walk back inside, and Dwayne spots Hildy on the dance floor. He stares at her for several seconds before approaching her.

"Here we go. I am Dwayne St. Thomas, and I can do this! Tonight's my night," he thinks to himself.

Dwayne looks in the mirror, fixes his hair, looks at his teeth, and likes what he sees.

"Oh yeah, it's on now!"

He approaches Hildy. She is wearing a short red skirt that doesn't leave much to the imagination.

"Hi Hildy girl...ummm, it's yo boy, Dwayne. I was wondering if you would slow dance with me," asks Dwayne.

Looking a bit annoyed and surprised, she replies, "Are you serious, St. Thomas. Have you been drinking? I smell it on your breath. My daddy told me that only bad boys' drink."

"Your daddy may be a coke dealer, but he's a smart man," Dwayne sputters. "I am all bad boy, Hildy. I have had four beers tonight."

Hildy melts as she looks at Dwayne.

"You drank four beers by yourself, Dwayne? Tell me, what kind of beers?"

"Glancers, babe."

"Really?" said an impressed Hildy.

"That's right, babe. That's 48 ounces, but who's counting?" Dwayne says, impressing himself with his quick math.

"Dwayne, nothing turns a girl on more than a guy who can drink multiple Glancers. My dad says 'Glancers are always the answer.' You want to dance with me, let's dance."

Hildy and Dwayne begin to slow dance. The song "Inspiration" by Chicago is playing. Hildy begins to rub the back of Dwayne's hair and gives him starry eyes, appearing as if a kiss is inevitable.

"Do you like this band, Chicago?" she asks. "I love the singer, Peter Cetera. Don't you?"

"Oh yes, Hildy. I enjoy his entire collection, especially the video for 'Stay the Night.' It moved me."

"I love that video!" she says, perking up. "Hey, I have a question: Would you jump onto a moving car for me like he did in the video?"

"You know it, babe!"

They rock back and forth and soon all the eyes in the gymnasium are on them. The quarterback taps the wide receiver on the arm.

"Who's this loser mowing our lawn?"

"It's that loser, Dwayne St. Thomas," chirps the running back as he walks up to his two teammates.

All three of the football players at once, "Well, shit."

The dance continues as Dwayne gets a little excited.

Hildy feels it pressing on her.

Giggling, she comments, "Wow Dwayne, you really are a bad boy."

"Sorry, Hildy. That thing has had a mind of its own. I'm sorry."

"Don't be. I'm almost 15."

The song continues when something begins to happen, and Dwayne's stomach begins making awful churning sounds. He is feeling ill and needs a bathroom. Beads of sweat begin to form along his hairline. He cannot wait for the song to be over.

"I'm gonna shit myself," he thinks. "Mother of God, I am going to shit myself."

The song finally ends.

"Thanks, Hildy. That was a nice dance," says a sweaty Dwayne.

All Dwayne wants to do is find a bathroom. He just doesn't need a toilet; he needs a toilet with a seat belt and a big warning sign outside stating: WARNING – BIOHAZARD. He tries to walk away, but Hildy grabs his arm and stares into his eyes.

"Not so fast, Dwayne S.T. I want a second dance. You would not tell a girl no, would you now?"

Dwayne is panicking, "Well, actually, I really need to..."

Just then, Hildy grabs Dwayne and kisses him as the song 'Free Bird' by the band Lynyrd Skynyrd begins playing.

"I love this song, Dwayne, and the best part is it is 14 minutes long. You're all mine, big boy!"

With this being his first kiss, he is overwhelmed and is unable to resist in any way. The dance continues, and

Dwayne's fate is now sealed. Dwayne's stomach continues to make awful noises. He sweats and sweats, and finally, he lets out a massive fart. As Ronnie Van Zandt sings, "Won't you fly high, free bird" and the music crescendos, his bowels give way and Dwayne, helpless, feels the shit rush out of him. He watches in horror as it spills down his legs and onto Hildy's shoes.

"Oh my god, what was that!" she screams. "What's that noise, that smell? Is that crud? Is that poo? Oh my god, Dwayne St. Thomas!" She says his name so loud, the entire gym can hear it. "I've been crapped on, Dwayne! You asshole, you shit on me!"

The music stops, and all eyes are on Dwayne, who is standing awkwardly, all frozen up like a deer caught in front of a truck's headlights. Dwayne's white shorts are a brown mess, and shit is dripping into his white loafers. Everyone is pointing at him.

Principle Pitts runs up to the stage and takes the microphone from the DJ. "Everybody be calm, Dwayne St. Thomas just shit his pants on Hildy. Please help Hildy to the restroom and get her cleaned up. Mr. St. Thomas, you will need to exit the gymnasium and think twice before returning to school on Monday." She then turns and looks at Larry. "Larry Dugan…get a mop."

Once he grasps the situation, he runs out of the gym into the parking lot, desperately looking for his bike and an escape. He is sweating bullets. Behind him, he leaves a bread crumb trail of brown shit droplets all the way from the spot of the explosion to his bike.

Back in the gym, the entire football team is laughing.

"Now that shit is funny," remarks the star wide receiver.

Back outside in the parking lot, it is beginning to drizzle. The liquid of the rain mixed with Dwayne's soiled self makes for an even drippier, soupier situation.

Dwayne approaches his bike. He has tears in his eyes. As he begins to pull away, he spots Rick walking toward him.

"Hey Dwayne, shitty night, huh?" he says as he laughs.

Dwayne doesn't say anything but simply stares at Rick. Confusion overtakes him. *What did Rick have to do with this?* he thinks.

As if reading his mind, Rick clears his confusion for him. "So good of you to have that fourth beverage with me. It's like my dad says, 'The fourth one always makes the difference,'" he says, giving a wink, and holding up the bottle of eye drops. "Sucker!"

Dwayne is startled. He stares at Rick as his white shorts are almost completely brown. He knows the truth; he knows what has happened. He was played by Rick. Putting eye drops in somebody's drink is a sure-fire way to make that person shit their pants. It was a common prank among the Glancerville youth over the years, commonly referred to as "The Dropper."

Dwayne is speechless, but worse, he is angry. However, he is in no position to respond or retaliate. He had shit all over himself, for Christ's sake! He knew he needed to flee the scene as quickly as possible. He begins peddling his bike away. "Better learn your place next time, loser!" he hears

Rick shout. The rain now begins to intensify as he rides off; shit is still dripping from his shorts and shoes.

Meanwhile, in the school gym, everyone is congregating and talking about the incident. Dwayne St. Thomas shitting his pants is the highlight of the evening.

The students are inventing name after name for Dwayne. It was here that "Dwayne, The Stain" was invented along with other long-running names such as "Shitty Pants," "Baron Von Poo," "Shitty Balls," "The Poo-nator," "The Shitter Man," and "Dr. Poo."

Principal Pitts, in her first year, is on top of the situation. Wasting no time and always eager to share the latest gossip, she walks to her office, picks up the phone, and calls the superintendent.

He answers the phone with a surprised tone.

"Well, hello, Claire. What do I owe the honor of you calling me after 9 p.m. on a Friday?"

"Hello, superintendent. I just wanted you to know that Dwayne St. Thomas, a sophomore at the high school, shit his pants while dancing with the prettiest girl in the school at the sophomore dance," she says.

"Who is the prettiest girl in the school?"

"Well, not that it should matter to a married man like yourself, sir, but it's Hildy MacMuphyn."

"Ah yes, I know the name. I do business with her father. So tell me, Principal Pitts, why are you at the sophomore dance?"

"I always attend these events to make sure everyone is safe. Plus, I date the DJ."

There is silence on the other end of the phone for several seconds and then finally a response.

"Um, okay, but don't you think you may be a little old to be dating the DJ, Principal Pitts? And as for tonight's episode with Dwayne St. Thomas, don't you mean, 'Dwayne The Stain?'"

He lets out an evil chuckle as he hangs up the phone.

Principal Pitts would go on throughout her career to always reference the Dwayne St. Thomas situation when dealing with her student body. She would often end her student body addresses with phrases such as, "Work hard, keep it honest, do not wind up a Dwayne St. Thomas," or another one was "Work hard, and good things will happen, and when at the dance, don't be crappin'!"

***

As Dwayne concludes his recollection for Dr. Gross, he lights another cigarette.

"Yep, that's how it all went down, Doc, and in a few days, it will mark 20 years."

Dr. Gross looks on in amazement.

"Wow, in all my years, I have never heard a story like that. May I have one of your cigarettes, Dwayne?"

Dwayne obliges and hands the doctor a smoke, lights it for him, and pushes the ashtray in the middle of the coffee table so they can share it. Dr. Gross takes a few big puffs before continuing the conversation.

"Now, while you may not like what I have to say, as a professional, it is my job to help clients, and part of it is telling them the uncomfortable truth. The thing is, Dwayne, you brought this upon yourself, you only have yourself to blame for it, and it is your burden to carry. I appreciate your honesty and wish you well, but anyway, I need to wrap things up. I have a 4:30 appointment."

Dwayne was expecting words of encouragement, methods of therapy and suggestions for personal improvement. Instead, he was being dismissed. Annoyed, he does not hold back. "Really, you suck, Dr. Gross," he remarks as he gets up and leaves the doctor's office. He gets into his Spark and drives off.

"Just doesn't seem worth the time and effort to me," he says to himself as he lights a Doral for the final 10 minutes of the drive.

CHAPTER 5

MESS IN MONTANA

Dwayne is just minutes away from home when he decides to make his usual stop by the Gasmart Station to buy an 18-pack of Glancers and say hi to his lady friend, Shelby. Dwayne and Shelby have been seeing each other off and on for a few months.

As Dwayne enters the station, he is greeted with a warm smile by his boo.

"Did you see your therapist today?" she asks.

"Just coming from there. I told Dr. Gross the whole damn story of the night I shit my pants."

"Wait, he didn't already know? I thought that was now required reading in his field."

Dwayne shakes his head. "It is, I think. I meant the story from my perspective. I can't recall remembering it from start to finish as well as I did in the therapy session I had with Dr. Gross today."

"Did you make any breakthroughs or progress?"

"No, he had another appointment to get to and pretty much kicked me out before offering any real advice."

"Damn, Dwayne," Shelby says, concerned. "Maybe he's fed up that you never show up for appointments and has given up on you. Do you have enough money left for follow-up visits? I thought your parents were still giving you money for these sessions."

"Well, babe, when I back out money for Glancers, Dorals, and the Landing Strip, there ain't much left."

Shelby gives Dwayne a disturbed look.

"You really need to clean it up, Dwayne. You are a mess. I need to get back to work. I'll see you tomorrow for our date."

Dwayne wraps up his visit with Shelby, puts his Glancers in the Spark, lights a smoke, and heads home. After a quick change of clothes, he heads over to the Landing Strip to meet Larry. His friend has a cold beer waiting for him as promised. Marie is bartending and greets Dwayne with her usual hug. A grumpy Dwayne starts the conversation hot.

"That damn Principal Pitts. I hate her."

"Well, hello to you too, Stain!" exclaims Marie.

"What did she do to you now?" asked Larry.

Dwayne takes a few strong sips of his Glancer and looks Larry dead in the eyes.

"Larry, do you know what day September 25 is, just short of two weeks from tonight?"

"Yeah, Dwayne, everyone knows what it is. It's the White Pants Festival. The festival Rick started about 10 years ago. The single biggest douchebag night of the year. Even douchebags that don't go out all year long go out for White Pants Festival. Like, if on New Year's Eve, 50 percent of douchebags were out, or on a normal Friday, 27 percent, damn near all 100 percent of them are out on White Pants Festival. It's like paying taxes for them. In order to be a douchebag in Glancerville, you *must* participate in White Pants Festival."

"That's great, Larry, but that is not what I was referring to."

A frustrated Dwayne goes back to drinking his beer while Marie begins chuckling behind the bar. She knows precisely what answer Dwayne was looking for.

"If White Pants Festival is mandatory for douchebags, how come you two never attend?" Marie jokes.

Larry notices that Dwayne is giving him the stink eye and tries to re-engage him in the conversation.

"Your silence tells me that there was something else you were referring to when it comes to September 25. I am all out of answers, Dwayne. Why don't you enlighten me?"

Dwayne remains silent.

Marie senses the situation and decides to rectify it.

"It's the anniversary of Stain shitting himself at the sophomore dance. Get with the program, Larry, you practically forced him into the damn situation. Of all people, you should remember what day September 25 is."

"Holy shit, it's been that long. That shit was legendary. Sorry, Dwayne, it must have stunk for you, no pun intended. It completely slipped my mind, pardon the expression," said Larry as he and Marie laughed out loud.

Dwayne does not find it humorous as he slams his bottle on the bar, turns to Larry, and looks him square in the eyes.

"It ruined my life, Larry. I have never been able to live it down. Throughout high school, no girl would talk to me. I was just 'Dwayne the Stain' or 'Shitty Pants.'"

"Don't forget 'Dr. Turd' and the 'Shit Monster,'" adds Larry.

"Baron Von Poo," added a random customer sitting four seats down at the bar.

"Thanks, buddy, I almost forgot," said Larry to the random customer.

Marie is listening to the conversation and feeling remorse at the sadness in Dwayne's demeanor. Marie and Dwayne grew up together. Although they went to different schools, they were close as kids. Dwayne asked Marie out on several dates over the years but Marie couldn't do it. She could not be the girl dating the guy who shit his pants at the dance. She has often felt guilty about that. She also feels guilty for her late-night hookups with Dwayne's brother, Dwight, during the years he was attending Glancerville University. Dwight treated Marie poorly and never respected or treated her with kindness the way Dwayne surely would have. Dwight would brag to others about the affair while Marie would deny it whenever around Dwayne. She did not want to cause poor Dwayne any more heartbreak.

"Maybe you should have moved away to get a fresh start, you know, like a fresh pair of boxers. It could have made a huge difference. You have been moping around this town for 20 years. Nowhere else in America do people know you crapped your white shorts at that damn dance while dancing with Hildy MacMuphyn."

"Not so sure about that, Marie," adds Larry, "I heard a couple of people talking about it when I was backpacking last summer in Colorado."

"Well, fewer people know, is what I meant."

Dwayne says nothing. Marie hands both Larry and Dwayne another beer.

"Last ones girls," she says. "We had a big group in here earlier, ran us straight out of Glancer. The next shipment comes on Tuesday."

"What the hell, Marie, that's bullshoot! That's four days," yells Dwayne.

Dwayne only drinks Glancer beer. He rarely, outside of an occasional shot, will ever delve into another beer. He is extremely brand loyal.

"Branch out, Stain, try something new. I'll give you a Glancer Dark. It will put some hair on your chest. These things just hit the market today, and Glancer Distribution is really pushing them. Apparently, the old man tried marketing these back in the day, but society was not ready, and now his grandkid is making up for the lost time. So have one and tell me what you think."

"Fine, but I'm not too happy about this dark beer crap, Marie. I might have to take my business elsewhere."

"Geez, Dwayne, say it ain't so, you and Larry drinking elsewhere. Whatever would a girl do?"

As Marie's hands Larry and Dwayne their first ever Glancer Dark, in the door walks a tall preppy kid with a fraternity baseball hat, sweater vest, and khakis. He was looking like an over-aged frat boy who has not been able to find any real meaning in life since college. You know the kind, the kid that is six years out of college but still wears the t-shirts and hats of the fraternity he joined. He sits at the bar about six seats over from Dwayne and Larry. Larry immediately senses the presence of a douchebag and gives him a look of disgust.

"I know that prick, Dwayne. He's bad news," said Larry.

"He looks about as suspicious as the backside of my balls," agrees Dwayne.

Marie approaches the newcomer as he takes his seat at the end of the bar.

"Hi honey, I have not seen you here before. What can I get you?"

He wastes no time in proving Larry and Dwayne's suspicions true.

"Your phone number and your best-selling beer," he replies.

Marie is not amused as she takes a step back.

"Excuse me, sir, I will get you a Glancer Dark, but as for my phone number, you got the wrong girl and the wrong bar and the wrong night."

Larry motions for Marie to come over to where he is sitting so he can talk to her privately after she delivers the beer to the gentlemen.

"Marie, the clown over there, I know who he is. Meet Montana, Lance Montana. He is a resident douchebag of several U.S. cities, and it appears as if he is making Glancerville his next target. He scams girls all over the city, steals their credit cards, runs up bar tabs, gets beat up at bars and frat parties, and is arrested twice a year. He is always on the move because he is such a scumbag, and now Marie, he has found the Landing Strip, your bar. This guy is such a sloppy turd. All you have to do is search for him on the internet. His bullshit is all over the Information Superhighway."

Montana, not hearing Larry, sits down and begins to drink his beer.

The topic of the 20th anniversary of the dance is recurring. Dwayne is more distraught tonight than usual, and it is obvious.

Larry tries to make him feel better.

"Stain, nobody can waive a magic wand or erase the past. You need to learn how to deal with this. It's been too long, buddy."

Dwayne appreciates the sentiment.

"I know, Lare-Bear, I know. Sometimes I just wish I could have some magical power to make it all go away and restore my life to what it was before the dance. But I know that sounds dumb."

Larry takes a sip of his beer and places his arm around Dwayne's neck.

"It's not dumb, Dwayne. All adults, even ones who didn't ruin their lives by shitting on the prettiest girl at school at the sophomore dance, wish they had a superpower from time to time. So, tell me, Dwayne, what would your superpower be if you could have one."

Dwayne lights a Doral and takes a few pulls on his beer. Then, after a couple of minutes of silence, he speaks.

"I'll answer that fucking question, Larry. If I could have one superpower, it would be the ability to make anyone I don't like shit their pants just by willing it. Then, all my enemies would know the humility I have felt the last 20 years."

Larry cannot believe what he has just heard. He removes his arm and stands up from his bar seat.

"That's dark, Dwayne, real dark. I mean, you have worse issues than I thought."

Dwayne says nothing in response. He and Larry sit in silence until Montana speaks. "Did you know I bought a new shirt and pants for White Pants Festival?" he asks.

Larry and Dwayne ignore Montana and continue talking as Marie reads all about his exploits on the internet.

Montana continues to ramble on, hoping that someone will listen and pay attention.

"And my dad got me in the VIP tent on Main Street. He knows the owner. He played for the Raiders in the 90s. I have a picture of us together at the White Pants Festival two years ago. Want to see?"

They continue to ignore Montana, but it's getting harder and harder. He's the kind of annoying that can't be replicated by normal people.

Marie hands Dwayne and Larry two more beers. She looks at Dwayne and asks, "What do you think? Is it changing your world, the Glancer Dark?"

"It's not so bad. It can't make this day any worse."

Larry is growing annoyed with Dwayne's self-pity party.

"Listen, Dwayne, you need to stop living in the past. Sure, you have had a shitty 20 years but look at you. You have a great job, you can drink more Glancers than anyone I know, and Shelby really likes you. Are y'all still going out from time to time?"

"I don't know, Larry. After Hildy, everything just doesn't seem right."

"Stop it, DST, that was two dances, 20 years ago, one kiss, and one huge shitting of the pants. I think your next relationship has room for improvement. You sitting around here chain smoking and drinking damn near a case of beer a night is not going to clean those white shorts and erase history. It's time to move on."

Montana chimes in again, "Did you know I was awarded the construction contract for the new buildings downtown that are going up? My dad...."

Larry interrupts. "Kid, not now! My friend is having a tough week!"

Two hours later, it was 1 a.m. Dwayne and Larry are at the bar, and four empty bottles are in front of them.

"Holy hell, this Glancer Dark has got a kick. I feel something I have never felt before. It's not even a drunken feeling. It's like something has come over me," said Dwayne.

"Well, maybe the Uber driver can figure it out for you," Marie says. "Last call boys. It's late, and I want to start counting my money."

Marie hands Larry and Dwayne their final beer, but they can barely even drink them.

Dwayne and Larry both begin to nod off at the bar but awaken several minutes later when they hear arguing between Marie and Montana.

"Sir, it's not your name on the credit card. I cannot run it. It is in a girl's name. You are out of luck without an ID matching the credit card."

"Did you know I know every attorney in Glancerville, and I will have this place closed down if you don't run this card? It belongs to my girlfriend."

"Why do you start off every sentence with 'Did you know'? You are a real weirdo. Sorry, sir, you'll have to find a different form of payment, or I'll call the cops."

"I would advise against that," threatened Montana.

Larry comes to Marie's defense,

"Hey kid, pay your tab or get the hell out of here."

Montana walks over to Larry. The tension thickens. "Did you know I'm going to kick your ass?" he says.

Then, Montana whales on Larry, knocking him to the ground. Dwayne doesn't know what to do. He starts panicking. Then something comes over him, and he begins to stare really hard at Montana. His eyes are twitching. All of a sudden, Montana shits himself. It comes flying through his shorts and onto the ground. He jumps up. He is startled. His hat is on the floor, covered in his own shit. It is running down his leg.

"Oh my God, oh my God," shouts Marie.

"This has never happened before!" Montana exclaims as he stares at his legs in horror. He's a mess. Suddenly, he takes his shorts off and runs out the door, wearing nothing but his soiled boxers. The smell is rank, to say the least.

Dwayne helps Larry up. Marie is laughing hysterically. "Did that really just happen?"

"What just happened? That kid was attacking me, and he just crapped his pants. Talk about being saved by the bell. Marie, that's enough, close us out," Larry says.

Marie is frantically looking for a mop.

"Never a dull moment when you two jackasses are in the bar."

Marie mops up Montana's mess and hands Larry and Dwayne their respective tabs.

Larry and Dwayne pay their bar tabs and walk out to the parking lot.

As they wait for their Uber, Dwayne turns to Larry.

"Larry, I have something to tell you, and I don't think you will believe it."

"What, Dwayne?"

"I think I made that kid shit his pants, I just stared at him, and I had this weird feeling that it was going to happen, and it did. Remember a few hours ago, when I said I wish I had that power, the power to make people shit their pants by looking at them? It's as if someone was actually listening to me."

Larry shakes his head and immediately puts this thought to rest.

"You're drunk, Dwayne."

"Maybe, but Larry, something was going on with that."

Larry is still not buying what Dwayne is selling.

"OK, Dwayne, make me shit my pants. Just do your thing."

"I don't think it works that way, Larry. It's like the Incredible Hulk, and I'm David Banner. I need to be possessed into doing it."

"The kid shit his pants, and it probably made you happy because it's the first known public shitting of pants in 20 years in this city," Larry says. "But to take credit for it is another thing, Dwayne. Our Uber is here. Let's go."

They share a ride back to the Lost Souls Lofts. It is a quiet ride as nobody is speaking. They finally reach their destination.

As they exit the car, Larry turns to Dwayne.

"I know that seeing another man crap himself probably gave you great relief, but DST, don't think about it too much. This is reality, and you do not have a superpower or any dumb-shit like that. Love ya, buddy, good night."

Larry walks off, leaving Dwayne alone in the parking lot with the neon lights of the Tainted Horse winking at him from across the street.

"Dwayne St. Thomas is here, girls. Hold onto your panties," he says to himself as he begins his walk across the street.

Dwayne walks into The Horse and sits at the bar. Strippers walk on the bar, stopping by each customer, and hustling for tips. The bar is a gigantic U-shape that seats 50 customers. Although there are tables and private sections, the bar walk is the cash cow for the women of the Tainted Horse.

The bartender approaches Dwayne and asks him what he would like to drink

"Just a Glancer, please."

"All we have is Glancer Dark," she replies.

"What the hell is going on in this town? Is everyone out of Glancer?"

"They are really pushing the Glancer Dark, baby. The distributor is asking their regulars to carry more than Glancer for a few weeks."

"Well, a Glancer Dark it is," Dwayne agrees.

Dwayne has a few beers and lights a smoke at the bar. He realizes it is probably time for his nightcap. He signals the bartender for one final beer and his check. Just then, a stripper walks up to him. "Hey, sugar," she says. "You want me to dance for you a little bit?"

"Sorry, I only have my debit card, and these Glancer Darks are $4 each. I'm almost tapped out."

Realizing she was not even going to get the obligatory $1 tip in the garter belt from Dwayne, she reacted accordingly.

"Loser, why would you even come here?"

She kicks his half-full bottle onto the floor. Dwayne is in disbelief.

"What the hell, sister?"

The stripper moves away and starts gossiping with customers three seats down. They start pointing at Dwayne. Dwayne realizes he is the butt of their jokes and wants to leave the bar right away. But he knows he can't go anywhere because he ordered another beer coming. And insult or not, Dwayne St. Thomas would never leave a beer behind.

"Hey Stain, what are you doing to celebrate the 20th?" yelled a random customer pointing at him with the offended stripper.

"I bet you ain't got shit to do, September 25," chimed in another customer.

Both customers and the stripper are laughing hysterically. Dwayne begins "the stare." The same feeling from the Landing Strip begins. His eyes twitch, and he's locked in. He stares down the stripper. Suddenly, she keels over and shits all over the bar, spraying the two hecklers. Shit flies everywhere. Projectile. It's a mess. The place is horrifying. Dwayne is in shock as this is the second time tonight that he has had this sensation resulting in pant shitting. He quickly runs out of the bar but is stopped by the doorman.

"Not so fast. Why are you running? Did you pay your tab? You're the loser that shit his pants at the sophomore dance in 2001, aren't you? Dwayne? That's your name, right?"

Dwayne is frozen, not sure what he should do.

"You are him, the Shit Monster. You defecated all over Hildy MacMuphyn."

Dwayne stares at the doorman once again with the same look and symptoms. Suddenly the doorman shits himself.

"Oh my god, I just soiled my pants!" he screams.

The soiled doorman needs to leave for obvious reasons, so he calls over the walkie-talkie.

"I need backup at door one. I have a customer I need to chase down. I'll be back in about 30 minutes."

The doorman runs off. Dwayne is sweating and scared. He begins to race back to his apartment. He's thinking about the night and mostly his wish. Did someone actually hear him? He made three people shit their pants in the last few hours. Perhaps luck was about to change for Dwayne St. Thomas.

"Holy shit, I knew it. It's real!"

Dwayne stumbles across the street as he returns home and enters his apartment. He takes two Glancers out of the fridge and opens them both while lighting a Doral. Dwayne is thinking about the events of the last several hours. It has been a surreal experience, to say the least. He knows there is something to it all but cannot piece it all together. He doesn't believe in magic powers or in anything extraordinary. He doesn't even watch Star Trek. But something unusual is going on. He finishes his first beer and opens the second. As he sips his final beer and smokes his final cigarette, he begins to nod off to sleep.

CHAPTER 6

PRIVATE GLANCER

After a long day and even wilder night, Dwayne is snoring on the couch as "Private Dancer" by Tina Turner is playing on the radio. His second Glancer is spilled on the floor as he just can't stay awake to finish it. It is not unusual for Dwayne to pass out on the sofa as he attempts to drink the unnecessary final beer after a long night at the bar. Suddenly, he is awakened by a loud knock on the door. He jumps up from his sleep with a confused and startled look on his face.

"Sweet almighty, it's 4 a.m. This had better be good, Larry," he grumbles.

Stumbling across his living room, Dwayne opens the door. To his surprise, it is not Larry, but an elderly gentleman in a top hat, wearing a suit and holding a six-pack of Glancer beer. Dwayne has a confused look in his eyes. Why on Earth would a stranger visit him at this hour and for whatever reason? Before Dwayne can say a word, the stranger beats him to the punch.

"May I come in, Dwayne? We have a lot to talk about."

Dwayne is rubbing his eyes and trying to figure out what the hell is going on. This stranger is not only at his front door, but he knows his name as well.

"Who the hell are you?"

Before awaiting an answer, Dwayne grabs the six-pack, opens a beer, and begins chugging it.

"I think you know who I am, Dwayne. Don't you recognize me from the picture at the Landing Strip?"

Dwayne scours his half-awake brain for a minute before recalling the picture from the Landing Strip of the older man. A picture he has stared at with amazement and awe for several years, dreaming of the day he would meet such a historical icon.

"No way, this must be a dream. It can't be you."

Seeing Dwayne's look of amazement, the man begins to speak again.

"I, Dwayne, am Conrad Glancer, creator of Glancer Beer, and I am visiting you in your dream. I think we have some things to talk about."

Dwayne shakes his head in disbelief and even goes as far as pinching himself a few times.

"Ouch!"

"Are you done, Dwayne?" asks Conrad.

"OK, yeah, I know this is a dream, that much is true. But why are you here?"

Conrad moves into Dwayne's living room and turns down the stereo. He directs Dwayne to have a seat on the sofa, and he takes a seat in the chair next to him.

"Dwayne, don't you know what happened tonight? Don't you know the power you now possess? I am here to talk to you about your newfound power. It's what you wished for, isn't it, Dwayne?"

Dwayne thinks back about the evening and remembers what he said to Larry about his superpower wish. He knows he is asleep and this dream will pass, so he decides not to hold anything back.

"Making people shit their pants by staring at them. But how did you know about that? I have dreamed about that power for 19 years, and it just happened tonight."

Conrad gradually stands up and points at Dwayne.

"You wished upon it in my presence. The Landing Strip was my bar for years. My spirit is there. I know how much you have been hurting the last 20 years, so when you told Larry you wished to have one power, the power to make your enemies shit their pants, I bestowed it upon you. It is yours, Dwayne, but you must use it wisely because time will run out on this power. You must even the score with all your enemies and do it soon. Not only that, you must do it smartly. Pardon the expression, Dwayne, but misuse of the power, and can we say, shit won't fly."

Dwayne, still in disbelief.

"I don't get it. How does my power work?"

Conrad sits back down, crosses his arms, and looks him squarely in the eyes.

"Those who have harmed you or wish you evil will be subject to your powers. Those who have been fair to you, you can still make shit themselves, but that's just not very cool. If they treat you poorly in your presence and bring up your mishap at the dance, you will simply give them the 'Glance of Disaster'. Oh, and you must have at least six Glancer beers in you for your powers to work. The more Glancers, the stronger your powers will be".

Dwayne listens in complete amazement.

"This is crazy. It won't work. If people keep shitting their pants around me, everyone will catch on. They will think I am drugging their drink like Rick did to me. It won't work, Conrad!"

Conrad opens a beer for himself. Before he continues, he bums a smoke from Dwayne.

"Say, Dwayne, can I have one of those donkey dicks to smoke, and do you have anything to munch on? I am hungry?"

Dwayne hands Conrad a smoke and lights it for him. He then goes to the kitchen and looks in the cupboard.

"All I have are crackers. Which kind do you want."

"Round or square, it doesn't matter," replied Conrad.

Dwayne brings the crackers over to Conrad and begins to speak again as he drags on his smoke.

"Dwayne, this is a special power. That is why you must be strategic and get more bang for your buck. Picking off all of your enemies one by one will take years. I suggest you go for the big payday, the big day to even the score with the hundreds of uptown and downtown snobs that have ruined your life for the last 20 years."

Dwayne's eyes open wide. He stares at Conrad.

"You don't mean...."

"Yes, Dwayne, it's exactly what I mean. Go big or go home."

Dwayne looks agitated.

"I hate that expression. It's so dumb. Don't people realize how much I like my home."

"You know I am right, Dwayne," Conrad replies.

Dwayne knows exactly the event which Conrad is referencing. The biggest night of the year in Glancerville.

"White   Pants   Festival?"   asks   Dwayne.

The White Pants Festival is a yearly occurrence in Downton Glancerville, where the arts district, primarily Main Street, has a block party event. Everyone dresses in white pants and black shirts and pretends to be cultural, drinking wine and looking at art. However, by 11 p.m., it officially becomes the biggest douchebag bar night in the city. Some people love the White Pants Festival. Others hate it. However, everyone would agree. It is the last night of the year anyone would want to shit their pants in public.

"Yes, Dwayne. What is a better time to get your revenge and use your power than White Pants Festival? It's only 12 days away so you must master your power between now and then. Dwayne, if done right, Main Street will be a shit show," he says with a laugh, the smoke curling around his face like a cloud.

Dwayne jumps off the couch as he wakes up from the dream. Sweat is pouring from his face, but for the first time in a long time, he feels good. Powerful, even. After 20 long years, Dwayne realized that he was now the card counter at the blackjack table and he was about to take down the casino.

"I can't wait to make people shit all over themselves," he whispers to himself.

Dwayne begins practicing his glance as he stares in the mirror. He incorporates hand motions and stylistic flair. He is a true superhero now. He just needs a name, a cape, and a uniform. Dwayne has never been more excited for the start of the next day.

"I'll be damned, White Pants Festival," he mumbles before nodding back to sleep.

As Dwayne nodded off, he began a separate dream. He is sitting in a chair with Tina Turner dancing around him, like in the video from 'Private Dancer.' However, in Dwayne's dream this particular night, the chorus is changed to "I'm Your Private Glancer."

CHAPTER 7
A DATE TO REMEMBER

Tonight, Dwayne has plans to take Shelby out on the town. They met a few months ago at the grocery store. Dwayne was buying a case of Glancer and a carton of Dorals. Shelby was behind him in the checkout line. She saw Dwayne panic when the cashier announced his total, $94, and she watched him hurry out of the store. He seemed ashamed.

Sensing this stranger was in desperate need of help, Shelby followed him into the parking lot and knocked on the window of his Spark. Dwayne rolled down the window. "Can I help you, sister?"

"You do know, sir, at the Gasmart Station around the block, you can get a case of Glancer and a carton of Doral's for just over $70. That would save you almost $24. And if you don't mind me saying, I bet a man like you could use an extra $24," she said. And with those words, Dwayne knew he had finally met someone special.

Shelby then gave her business card to Dwayne. It read: "Shelby McGhee. Head Cashier. Gasmart Glancerville East."

"Whoa, I have never met a woman in oil and gas before," he said. Shelby winked at Dwayne and walked away. The Gasmart Station has been Dwayne's regular stop ever since.

Ready for today's date, Dwayne pulls up to the Gasmart Station in the Spark.. He is dressed nicely, and his hair is slicked back. He is singing along with the song on the radio. Dwayne is feeling good. He gets out of the car and walks into the store to see Shelby counting money and getting ready for a shift change. He has a swagger that he has frankly never had. He is a changed man.

He looks straight at Shelby, extends his arm, and points at her.

"How's my best girl doing?"

A surprised and shy Shelby responds. "Hey, Stain, you look nice today, coming from a funeral?"

"Quite the opposite, Shelby. Perhaps it is more appropriate to say I am coming from birth, or a re-birth if you will," he chuckles.

"Oh, do tell."

Dwayne hops up on the counter and rests his legs on the trash can.

"Babe, let's just say Glancerville is running out of time to kick ol' Dwayne St. Thomas around anymore. The year of Dwayne is quickly approaching. Do you mind if I grab a six pack of Glancers from the walk-in? This whole damn town has been out of them the last couple of days. My own personal inventory is nearly depleted. Everyone is on this Glancer Dark kick."

"Sure, go ahead, Dwayne."

Shelby returns to counting money as Dwayne walks to the cooler and grabs a six-pack of his favorite beer. Right next to the six-pack of Glancer, he sees a six-pack of Glancer Dark. He stares at it and shakes his head.

"Glancer Dark, what a bunch of crap."

Dwayne opens a Glancer and walks back toward the register.

"Come on, Shelby, I'm taking my girl out. Let's try that new diner on the service road. Nothing is too good for my girl."

Shelby, startled by the new Dwayne, blushes.

"Gee whiz, I like Dwayne St. Thomas 2.0. Are you still driving that sexy Chevy Spark?"

"Electric window control, tape deck and a CD player, babe," he answers with a smile. "Let's roll."

The happy couple exit the Gasmart and enter the Spark. Dwayne lights a smoke as he fires up the engine and puts a CD in the player.

"How about a little magical music by Dirty Urine?" he asks, as their hit song 'I Love Yellow' begins.

"Oh DST, you really know how to get a girl going, I love Dirty Urine. They are headlining White Pants Festival this year.".

"I have been thinking, Shelby, we should play up our game. People kick us around and make fun of some dumb shit from 20 years ago. We can't let it bother us. Time for us to evolve."

Shelby stares at Dwayne for a few seconds. "You shit your pants at the high school dance, Dwayne. I didn't," she says carefully. "They don't kick me around. They kick you around. You have been running from your past all these years. It's so sad, Dwayne, you are a victim of bullying, mainly by that creep Rick Townsend."

Dwayne is not giving in to pity or criticism on this day. "Apples and oranges babe. Well not no more, Shelby. By the way, do you own any white pants?"

Shelby replies with a confused look.

"Why do you ask? You are not thinking of going to White Pants Festival, are you?"

"That I am Shelby, my love, that I am."

An annoyed look comes across Shelby's face as she takes the cigarette out of Dwayne's mouth and tosses it out the window.

"White Pants Festival is for rich people if that is what you are referring to. I have no interest in attending that festival, Dwayne, and quite frankly, I have no idea why you would either. It is packed full of the same people who have been making fun of you since Rick started it 10 years ago."

"Nonsense Shelby, we'll get you some white pants. There's a TJ Maxx on the way. I'm taking you to White Pants Festival next Saturday, babe. Gonna check out the art, drinks, and music on Main Street. I may even add a few strokes of genius to the portraits myself."

Shelby is confused by Dwayne's tone. Normally she knows a beaten down and somber Dwayne. Something is different today.

"Count me out, Dwayne, take Larry and that whore Marie. I refuse to ever attend an event hosted by Rick Townsend, and frankly, I am shocked you would either after all he has done to you."

Shelby McGhee is a simple girl from North Glancerville, a suburb also known as the gateway to the world because the airport is located there. She grew up in a very strict family with nine brothers and sisters. She has been with Gasmart for over 12 years. She does not drink or smoke, so she is often concerned about Dwayne's constant consumption of Glancer beer.

"How many Glancers have you had today, Dwayne?" she asks, her voice tinged with concern.

"Five, babe," he says breezily. "Need one more for sure."

"What does that mean?"

"In due time, babe, in due time."

"What are the most Glancers you have ever had in one day?" she asks.

"35."

"Geez, Dwayne, that's a lot of Glancers."

"I'm a lot of man."

Dwayne and Shelby drive another few minutes and finally arrive and park at the diner. Dwayne turns to Shelby.

"Don't worry, Shelby, you are with me. Nothing bad will happen to you on my watch. Let's go get some food."

The couple walks in and has a seat at the counter. It's more of a truck stop kind of diner than a traditional one. It has counter seating with a few tables spread around the place. There is an old-style jukebox and cigarette machine for decor. After several minutes the waitress approaches them.

"Hey there, you two. Never seen y'all in here before. Welcome, here are some menus. Let me know when you are ready."

Without hesitation, Dwayne speaks up.

"I'll start with a Glancer, and the lady will have a coffee."

Shelby stares at Dwayne. Partly offended by Dwayne ordering for her but, once again, partly impressed with the newly confident Dwayne.

"Wow, Dwayne, look at you, ordering for me. What if I would have wanted orange juice instead."

"Nonsense Shelby, I know what's best for you."

The waitress returns with the drinks and is ready to take their order.

"I'll have the Number One, over easy, extra bacon, and the lady will have the fruit cup. You need to keep that figure, babe."

Shelby, again startled, speaks up.

"Wow, Mr. Confidence, I may just miss the old Dwayne St. Thomas. This new guy is kind of an asshole. Ordering for me, worrying about my figure. Have you looked in the mirror lately, Dwayne? You are no Tom Selleck. I think I may miss the old Dwayne St. Thomas."

Dwayne lights a cigarette as he sips his beer, his sixth.

"The old Dwayne, he's gone, baby. He belongs to the streets now."

"Oh geez," mumbles Shelby.

Just then, in walks a husky older guy. He exchanges pleasantries with a few locals and tips his cap to the waitresses before making his way toward Dwayne and Shelby. The stranger gets just a couple of feet from the table and pauses.

"Excuse me, sir," he says. "You are in my seat. I am going to need to ask you to move. I wouldn't want to risk someone shitting their pants all over my favorite stool, no pun intended. I come here every day so beat it, pal."

Dwayne doesn't flinch. He takes a long drag of his Doral and a sip of his Glancer and then calmly stands up, putting his face about two inches from the rude man.

"What did you say?"

"I said, you need to get out of my stool, Dr. Poo!"

Shelby stands up and gets in between the two.

"Stop this, boys, Dwayne, let's just move."

Dwayne is not having it.

"It's OK, Shelby. I don't know if this cowboy knows who he is messing with. And I sure as shit don't think he brought a big enough lasso."

Dwayne takes his beer and drinks down the last swallow.

"Tell me one more time who you think you are speaking to."

"Dwayne, stop," pleads Shelby.

"I'm talking to Dwayne St. Thomas, the shitting his pants legend of Glancerville. The loser who soiled himself at the sophomore dance while dancing with Hildy MacMuphyn. To 'Free Bird' of all songs! Now move it, boy."

Dwayne has had enough. He knows it is time for this gentleman to witness the powers of DST. He begins to stare. Nothing happens. He is trying and trying, but nothing is working.

"Why are you staring at me and making these weird faces, boy?"

Dwayne continues. He is trying to call upon his power. He knows he has had the six Glancers that Conrad mentioned were necessary. It is simply not working.

"All the hell with it. It's time for me to take my stool the old-fashioned way, by kicking your ass."

The diner man throws Dwayne on the floor and starts kicking him. He picks him up by his hair and throws him out the door. Shelby comes chasing behind, screaming.

"What do you think of me now, Stain? You messed with the wrong regular!"

He continues to beat Dwayne, throwing him onto the hood of the Chevy Spark. He then begins kicking the side door, causing it to dent.

"My Spark! No, not my Spark," pleads Dwayne.

The man stops kicking the car and Dwayne's ass. He takes a deep breath and looks at Dwayne.

"I'll take care of the check, Shitty Pants. Don't let me catch you in these parts again."

The man turns and heads back inside, leaving Dwayne on the ground, bruised and bloody.

Shelby runs over to Dwayne and puts him in her arms right there in the parking lot. He is visibly distraught after getting the crap beat out of him. His powers have failed him.

"My poor baby," says Shelby.

"I can't believe it," replies Dwayne.

"What, Dwayne, you have been getting your ass kicked for 20 years? What did you think was different today? Why did you stand up to him? What has gotten into you in the last 24 hours? This isn't you."

"I've been lied to! Conrad, you lied to me!" he screams.

Shelby is confused and asks who Conrad is. But before Dwayne can answer the question, he lets out a subtle juicy fart.

"Ew, Dwayne, did you just shart?"

"Yes, Shelby, I just let a wet fart go, and now my pants are soiled."

She helps Dwayne up. There is a little brown stain on the rear of his pants.

"I'll clean that ass up, Dwayne. It will be OK."

They proceed to get into the Spark and drive off. It was not the date Dwayne was expecting.

CHAPTER 8

A WIN FOR THE LITTLE PEOPLE

Shelby drives Dwayne back to the Gasmart Station to get her car. Dwayne still can't believe it. How did his powers work yesterday and then end up failing him at the diner?

"Did I only drink five Glancers?" Dwayne thinks to himself, knowing damn well he had the full six. He decides to take out his frustration the way he always does, at The Landing Strip.

The bar has a long, proud history in the St. Thomas family. Dwayne's father, Dr. John St. Thomas, used to drink there. One night in the late '70s, he met the future mother of Dwayne St. Thomas, Jennifer. Jennifer and John fell in love at the Landing Strip as they completed medical school and dreamed of their life together. Over the years, the bar has been in a bit of decline, much like all of Glancerville East. Instead of being frequented by young professionals making their way up in the world, it sees the likes of Dwayne, Larry, and many others just trying to make it one day at a time. Occasionally a respected member of society, such as Rick or Hildy, will still show their face just for old times' sake.

Dwayne's parents never brought him to the Landing Strip because of the incident and guilt by association. However, back in the day, Dwight St. Thomas was a regular. The bar even named a burger and a drink special after Dwight. Many a winter's night Dwight St. Thomas would leave the bar with a woman on each arm and a jealous Marie behind the bar, knowing she was just his college fling..

Dwight has an "It" factor. Every guy wanted to be like him, and every girl wanted to be with him. Dwight was also quite the Glancer drinker as well. He once drank 65 Glancers on a single flight from Los Angeles to New York in his wilder days. There was little Dwayne could do to fill those shoes.

Dwayne's first night at the bar came several years after his parents and Dwight stopped going. Since then, he has been a regular and has befriended all the bartenders, especially Marie. He'll never forget when he first saw Marie at the Landing Strip.

xxx

She approached him as he sat at the bar. "Are you Dwayne St. Thomas? Do you remember me from when we were kids? You're the one who shit his pants at the dance a few years ago?

Dwayne looked down in his usual embarrassed look. He said nothing.

"It's ok. I hate Hildy MacMuphyn. You are a real man for shitting your pants while dancing with her. She deserved it by making you dance to 'Free Bird.' You are a hero to a lot of us. I went to a different school, but I was there that night."

xxx

Since that day, Marie and Dwayne have rekindled their childhood friendship, and a solid bartender-customer bond quickly formed.

Dwayne enters the bar looking pissed off and Marie quickly takes notice.

"Whoa, Stain, what happened to you?" she asks as she hands him a Glancer. "We re-stocked the original Glancer. You should be happy. No more of the dark beer for you."

"Take that picture down, Marie," he responds, pointing at the framed shot of Conrad Glancer on the wall. "Guy is full of shit."

"Um, how drunk are you, Stain? He died many years ago."

"Well, he is dead to me as of last night."

Just then, Rick walked into the bar. Obviously, there was no love lost between Rick and Dwayne over the last 20 years. Rick was a friend of Dwayne's when they were younger, but the friendship ended as days moved to months and months to years. Rick fell in with the "cool" kids who picked on and bullied Dwayne as much as they could. He was well-experienced with the ladies and excelled in every sport. He was the spitting image of Dwight St. Thomas. While he had friends, Dwayne was still a bit socially awkward through his grade school days, and Rick let him know it. Dwayne blames Rick for ruining his life. That is why Dwayne loved Conrad's idea about ruining Rick's annual summer event. He never apologized to Dwayne for putting the eye drops in the beer and worse, denies doing it. Rick went on to date Hildy the later years of high school and throughout college, and they seemed to have a perfect life.

"Hey, Dwayne, how's your night?" asks Rick in an unusually pleasant tone.

"Dwayne? You called me Dwayne. Having a bad day, Rick, you childhood-stealing piece of shit?"

"Ha ha ha, you don't mean that old buddy. A round of Glancers, Marie. Hey Stain, no hard feelings. Sorry about ruining your life. Can we call it even? I have had a hell of a day. Marie, put Stains beers on my tab tonight."

"Wow, Rick and Dwayne are hanging out. Who would have thought? Gee, Rick, you just apologized for ruining Dr. Poo's life. I could have sworn that sounded like an admission of putting the eye drops in his beer."

"Never, never. I would not do such a thing. My mom raised me Catholic, for Christ's sake!"

"So, what's eating your ass tonight, Rick," asked Dwayne.

Rick looks down at his beer for a moment before speaking. Finally, he gets the courage to say what's on his mind.

"It's Hildy. She is seeing some other dude. He is completely using her. Charging all of his crap to her credit card. She denied it for the longest time, but it was obvious when I saw her credit card statement. Khaki short pants, goofy baseball caps, oversized sunglasses, Widespread Panic concert tickets, sleeveless fleeces, button-down shirts, Coors Light. All these charges for things Hildy would never buy and are clearly for some jerk who can't stand on his own two feet."

"Sucker," laughs Dwayne.

"Where did she meet him?" asked Marie, "And I assume you are separated."

"I guess he got in a fight with Larry the other night and ran out of here. He met Hildy in the parking lot of our building. He just took a shower and changed clothes after he left here. He must have been bloody. Some girl had just kicked him out of her apartment and was yelling something about him running up her credit card. He looked like he did not have a place to go, and Hildy felt bad for him. The next thing you know, they are doing the 'no pants' dance.

Dwayne looks up with a grin.

"Shit, it was that guy."

"Montana!" exclaimed Marie.

"That's him," confirmed Rick. "That's his name, Lance Montana."

"He wears a goofy fraternity hat and a sweater vest and he always starts off every sentence with a question like 'What would you do', or 'Did you know'?'" adds Marie.

"Montana!" repeats Dwayne.

"He's taking her to White Pants Festival. My favorite night of the year, and she's going with that guy. It's my party, and she is crashing it. I'm so bummed. I even booked Dirty Urine as the headliner.

Dwayne's attention switches back to his power failure of earlier. "I had big plans for that night too, but not anymore," he says sadly. "Let's order shots."

"How about three Jaeger Root Beers?" asks Rick.

"I think you mean 'mini bombs'" replies Marie.

She prepares the shots and takes them to Rick and Dwayne. They toast and raise their glasses. Slamming them down, Rick looks at Dwayne and puts his hand on his shoulder.

"So, Stain, what were your big plans for White Pants Festival? I mean, no offense, but I didn't think they would allow your kind to attend events in the artsy part of town. It's for the accomplished, snobby people of the city, the ones that think they are elite, not high school losers like you. Again, no offense, though."

"Things were turning around, Rick, but I was made some false promises. Now I need to figure it all out. Don't count me out yet. I just hope Dirty Urine plays 'Bacteria Not My Fault.' That song rocks."

"Oh, I have counted you out for 20 years, St. Thomas."

Larry enters the bar and approaches Dwayne and Rick.

"Hey Rick," he says loudly. "I just saw Hildy getting T-Boned by that Montana guy in the parking lot of the Tainted Horse. Better go get your girl. She's looking like community property again, buddy. I'm parched. Hey, Marie, can you put me in for a Dwight the Legend burger, some fries, and an ice-cold Glancer."

Rick frowns. "Shut up, Larry. Screw you and the Stain. Take Stain's beers off my tab, Marie." He slams the remainder of his beer and flips off Dwayne and Larry as he throws $30 on the bar and walks out.

Larry and Dwayne smile as they see a defeated Rick walk out the door. A win for the little people at long last.

"Ok, Dwayne, I got your text. I'm here, so what did you want to talk to me about?"

Dwayne proceeds carefully. He knows his friend is already skeptical. "Larry, remember last night when I told you that I thought I had power when I made that Montana kid shit his pants?"

"Dumb as hell, but yes."

Dwayne takes a sip of his Glancer and lights a Doral.

"You know you can't smoke in here, Dwayne," yells Marie.

Dwayne ignores Marie, takes a few drags of the smoke, and crushes it out.

"Well, I went to the Tainted Horse afterward and made two more people who made fun of me shit their pants and then I went to sleep. Conrad Glancer came to me in a dream and told me he had bestowed a power on me, that all the people who made fun of me I can make shit their pants if I have six Glancers in me, and stare at them. So, I woke up today, took Shelby to a diner, drank six Glancers, and some dude bullied me. I went to make him shit, and the power wasn't there. I got my ass kicked, Larry. What do you think?"

Marie immediately stops what she is doing.

"First off, Stain, I can hear you from over here, and secondly, don't ever repeat that dumb story again. We may need to cut you off for good. Special powers, Conrad Glancer, making people crap their pants. Your brain is fried, Stain."

Larry adds, "Really, Dwayne, you saw someone other than yourself shit their pants, that Montana kid. It had nothing to do with you. Even if, and I am not saying it happened, two more people at the Tainted Horse shit their pants that night, it is merely a coincidence. Get a grip, Dwayne. Conrad Glancer, a dream. You're killing me, man."

"No one believes me," says a defeated Dwayne.

"Exactly, no one," chimes in Marie. "Look, Stain, why don't you focus your attention on Shelby. She's a nice girl. It's '$1.99 a Gallon Week' at Gasmart, so imagine how busy she is. Why don't you send her some flowers and get your   head   out   of   your   ass."

"Yeah, Dwayne, and no more talk of White Pants Festival. It's not for you," says Larry.

"No, Larry, I am going to White Pants Festival, and I'd like you and Marie to come with me. It may just be one hell of a show if I can figure a few things out in the next couple of days. Plus, Dirty Urine is heading."

"God, I hope they play 'Golden Shower Hour,'" Larry says. "I love that song."

"I'll go with you, Dwayne," says Marie. "Nothing happens in this bar on White Pants Festival, so I'm sure I can join you. Any chance your brother Dwight is coming into town for it."

"Why would you ask that?"

"Never mind, just curious."

"I'm in too," Larry says. "You haven't been enthusiastic about attending anything in 20 years, so I guess I should be supportive. I don't know what you're cooking up, Dwayne St. Thomas, but it smells like a turd."

Larry and Dwayne have a few more Glancers and call it a night. They both hop into the Uber they are sharing on their way home.

"Man, long day of getting my ass kicked and beer drinking," Dwayne says.

Larry nods in agreement. "Say Stain, how about a nightcap at the Tainted Horse."

"Not tonight, Larry. I'm broke, and I need to figure out how to get my powers back in full effect."

They arrive at their apartment complex and go to their respective units. Dwayne lights another smoke, grabs his usual two Glancers, and sits on the couch.

He again thinks back to the fateful night that forever changed his life. The night of his sophomore dance.

xxx

Dwayne arrived home on his bike, a shitty mess. He cannot fathom the situation that just occurred. He had been crying the entire ride home... and itching. He really grew a new appreciation for toilet paper that fateful evening. All he wanted was to get in his house, shower, and change clothing without his parents or Dwight noticing. No such luck. As he made the right-hand turn into his driveway, he saw several people on his patio. Dwight was throwing a party, and all his high school friends from years earlier were in attendance. There was a strong stench of beer and marijuana cigarettes.

"Shit, I am busted," Dwayne thought.

He ditched his bike behind a nearby tree. As he tries to sneak into the garage, Hildy's older sister, Dana, spotted him.

"Oh my God, Dwight, your little brother is all covered in shit. Wasn't he supposed to be at the dance tonight?"

The music stopped, and everyone turned toward Dwayne. Dwight approached and stared him up and down.

"You walk into my party, smelling and looking like a diaper and embarrass me in front of my friends. Look what you did to my white short pants," he said angrily.

Dwayne was shaking in fear and embarrassment.

"Go to the house and clean yourself up, sleep in the garage, and consider yourself unwanted," ordered Dwight.

He then turned to the crowd. "Sorry, everyone, he's adopted. Let's start the music back up and enjoy the evening."

Dwayne walked into the house. His parents were asleep. He walked quietly upstairs and stripped off all his clothes. He sat for several minutes on the toilet with his head down, crying and thinking about the night.

Meanwhile, back at the party, Dana MacMuphyn approached Dwight.

"Um, my sister just beeped at me, Dwight, so your shitty brother, he crapped himself at the sophomore dance while dancing with my sister. Not only that, Dwight, they were dancing to 'Free Bird'. He's gross. The St. Thomas family is ruined in this town if he remains in it and associated with you. Totally gross, Dwight. You have a reputation to protect. You own this town. That brother of yours has got to be dealt with."

"Don't worry, Dana. Dwayne will never be allowed to associate with my family. Wait until I tell Mom and Dad."

Dwayne emerged from the shower, put on his pajamas, and dialed Larry's number. It was late, and Larry's mother answered.

"Is Lare-Bear there?"

"Dwayne, it's after 11. Larry is still at the dance."

"Sorry, ma'am, can you just have him call me tomorrow?"

She paused and replied, "I'm sorry, Dwayne, you shit all over Hildy MacMuphyn at the sophomore dance. Larry has a future to think about. Maybe you should consider giving him a little bit of distance."

A dejected Dwayne hung up the phone and collapsed in bed. All through the night, the incident replayed in his head over and over.

The next morning, Dwayne opened his eyes and saw his parents opening up his window shades to let the light in . He sat up.

"Good morning, Dwayne," his mother began.

"Hi, Mom. I guess Dwight told you about last night."

"He did, and we are really disappointed in you, Dwayne. What made you think you could shit all over Hildy MacMuphyn at the sophomore dance?"

Dwayne's father interjected. "You know Dwayne, her father, is the biggest cocaine dealer in the city. We cannot afford enemies like that. We are respected doctors."

"I'm so sorry, Mom and Dad. I never meant to disgrace the St. Thomas' name."

"Well, Dwayne, you did, and we will need you to sleep in the garage until the end of high school. That's just a little more than two years."

"Yeah, Dwayne," added his father. "We will bring you food and water and take care of your arrangements to and from school. But we cannot have you in the house or even in public with us, no restaurants, and unfortunately, we will not be able to take you to the Landing Strip when you turn 18 like we planned."

Dwayne felt lower than all hell.

"I feel like I ruined everything last night. I am so sorry. What can I do to make it right?"

Jennifer and John look at each other and then back at Dwayne.

"Dwayne, you cannot turn back the clock, but there is good news," said his mom.

"Thank goodness, I need good news. What is it? Please tell me."

"We have Dwight, Dwayne. He will carry on the family legacy. Thank God for him. He never shat his pants at the sophomore dance."

xxx

The memory of that awful morning still stings Dwayne. Frustrated, he lights a Doral, lays back on the sofa, and looks at the ceiling.

"Talk to me, Conrad. Tell me where I go from here."

CHAPTER 9
CODE DWAYNE

It is September 20, just five days before White Pants Festival. Dwayne pulls up to the Gasmart Station. He cracks open a Glancer in the parking lot and drinks it quickly. He finishes it and opens another one. It's been a long few days for him. Conrad Glancer never visited him again in his dreams. He still has no idea how to activate his powers. What was the difference between the night it happened and the last few days? He knows he is easily meeting his quota of six Glancers, some nights even by a multiplier of three.

He walks into the station and sees Shelby behind the counter. It is the first time Dwayne has seen Shelby since he got his ass kicked by the guy in the diner and then sharted in the parking lot.

"Well, hey there, Shelby," he smiles awkwardly. "How's your day? Thanks for cleaning me up the other day. Sometimes I just don't know what gets into me."

"Well, usually it is a bunch of Glancers, but Dwayne, it's ok. We all shart from time to time. I see you are already into the Glancers today. It's only 2 p.m., Dwayne. Slow down."

Dwayne finishes the Glancer and lights a smoke. Shelby frowns. "You really need to stop smoking at gas stations, Dwayne."

"First smoke of the day, babe, and that was just my sixth Glancer. Do you want to see a movie when you get off? It's a $10 Glancer bucket night at the drive-in, and they have

'The Notebook' playing. I love that damn movie. It cracks me up!"

Shelby thinks for a few moments. '$1.99 a Gallon Week' really took a lot out of her, and she has been working nonstop.

"Maybe Dwayne, I have another few hours. Dottie called in sick. She's got a case of the shits real bad. She's been drinking a lot of the Glancer Dark. Blames it on that."

"That beer is the devil's drink," said Dwayne, as Lance Montana strolls in. He walks around aimlessly and suspiciously. Dwayne spots him.

"Montana!" he calls.

"I remember you from the other night," Lance says. "What would you do if you shit your pants in public? How embarrassing. I was going to kick your friend's ass."

Shelby chimes in. "Well, you are certainly asking the right guy, sir. So, Mr. Montana, what can I do for you"?

"I need to put some gas in my girlfriend's car. It's not my week, my credit card expired. I have no way to pay. Can you spot me? I will pay it next week."

"Sorry, sir, it doesn't work that way."

"Did you know I know everybody at Gasmart Corporate? If you keep treating me with this disrespect, I will call their lawyers and have you fired."

"Wow, Montana, you are such an asshole," says Dwayne.

Hildy walks in, dressed to the nines as usual.

"Come on, baby, just use my credit card. I trust you. As a matter of fact, you can keep it in your wallet for emergencies. I know you aren't going anywhere. I don't care what the internet says about you."

"I love you, babe?"

"Unbelievable," sighs Dwayne.

Hildy turns her attention to Dwayne.

"Hey, Stain. First off, I do not appreciate you smoking in the gas station. All these years later and I still cannot escape your toxins. Anyway, did you hear Rick and I broke up? Lance Montana is my new man. He owns all the contracts for the new construction in downtown Glancerville. He also knows several famous people in the NFL. You will treat him with the utmost respect when he sees you with your lowlife friends."

Just then, as everyone was engaged in the conversation, two men in ski masks walked in the front door of the Gasmart Station with clear intent on robbing the joint. There is about to be trouble.

"Did you know—"

"Everybody shut the hell up, this is a robbery," one of the masked men yelled. They turned toward Shelby. "You, behind the counter. Get all the cash in a bag. I want all your cigarettes too. The rest of you, get in the walk-in cooler, and don't make a peep. Give me your cell phones too!"

Shelby is panicking. She begins shaking, and tears are coming down her face. This is her first robbery in her oil and gas career.

"Get a hold of yourself, Shelby. All of our lives are in your hands, don't screw this up," encourages Dwayne.

"Oh, my god. Oh, my god," she yells as she presses the security button behind the counter, a direct line to the police.

Montana, Hildy, and Dwayne hand over their cell phones and jog over to the walk-in cooler. As he nears the door of the cooler, Dwayne turns and stares at the robber, hoping to make them shit, but nothing happens. He tries again. No luck. His powers have apparently left him just as fast as they arrived.

They enter the walk-in as Shelby frantically begins to try to empty the register. "Open the safe too. We want it all," says the other robber as he points a gun at Shelby.

Meanwhile, back in the walk-in, Dwayne is standing on boxes to see what is happening at the front of the store.

"They got a gun pointed at her. Are any of you packing?"

"Did you know—"

"Shut up, Montana! What am I going to do."

Dwayne turns and stares at the beer. He grabs a Glancer but then sees the Glancer Dark next to it. He remembers the night when he had no other choice but to drink Glancer Dark at the Landing Strip. He recalls that just after that, Montana shit his pants. He then thinks about immediately after when he went to the Tainted Horse and once again was forced to drink Glancer Dark. The stripper and bouncer would then crap themselves as well. "Well, I'll be damned," Dwayne says to himself. "Could Glancer Dark have been the beer that bestowed the power?"

He reaches for a Glancer Dark. At the front of the store, one of the masked men screams at Shelby to hurry up. Shelby is crying hysterically while the masked men are harassing her.

"You have 60 seconds, sister, hurry up, or your career in oil and gas is going to be a short one."

Dwayne hears a faraway siren. Help is on the way, but will it get here in time? Quickly, he downs the first, then the second, and then cracks open the third

"What in hell, Stain, your girl is getting robbed, and you are acting like you are at a fraternity hazing. I think you may have a damn problem," says Hildy.

Montana grabs a Glancer.

"You know, I wouldn't want you drinking alone Dwayne."

Montana pounds two Glancers alongside Dwayne.

"I like your style, Dwayne. Let the girlfriend handle the robbery, and we will just enjoy a couple of ice-cold brewskies."

"Stop talking to me. I'm working."

He proceeds to pound the next three beers. He reaches for the sixth.

"Don't let me down, Conrad," Dwayne announces as he twists off the top, the sirens growing louder.

"What? Who is Conrad?" asks Hildy.

Just then, three police officers pull into the parking lot. Panicked, one of the robbers pulls Shelby from across the register and puts the gun to her head.

"Stay back, coppers. If any of you try to stop us, or so much as move an inch, she is dead meat."

The police stand their ground outside. It is an official standoff. They are pleading with the robbers not to hurt anyone inside.

"Let the girl go. We understand you have Dwayne St. Thomas in there. Give us the girl and do what you want to him."

In the walk-in, Dwayne is racing vigorously toward finishing his sixth Glancer Dark.

"Did you know they are about to shoot your girlfriend in her head?" asks Montana.

Dwayne turns the Glancer Dark up and chugs it like no beer has ever been chugged before. He lets out a huge belch, lights a Doral, and looks at Hildy and Montana.

"Stay here, you two. It's not safe out there. I am going into action."

Dwayne emerges from the walk-in, takes a few steps forward, and stares at the two gunmen. The twitches return, all the signs, it's working. As he puffs on his Doral, he hears Conrad Glancer's voice ringing in his head.

"Do it, Dwayne. Make me proud. And I am sorry that I left out the dark beer part the other night in the dream."

One of the robbers notices Dwayne.

"What the hell, cowboy? Get back in the cooler, or all of you die."

Just then, Shelby lets out a loud, violent scream.

"Oh my God, I am going to shit my pants."

Poop shoots out from under her skirt. It hits one robber in the eye, and he falls to the floor and throws up. The other robber backs off.

"Holy shit, you are so gross! You just crapped all over us in mid-robbery."

"Oops, sorry, Shelby, wrong target. I'm still learning," chuckles Dwayne. Then he focuses his attention on both robbers, who each shit their pants within moments.

As the robbers roll around in their poop-soaked pants, the police storm in. Dwayne can't stop. He stares the police down, and all three officers shit themselves like crazy. Hildy and Montana emerge from the walk-in.

"What the hell is going on here?" asks Hildy.

Dwayne stares down Hildy and Montana. They both shit all over themselves.

"Did you know that's twice in one week?" whines Montana.

Hildy is beside herself; she has defecated all over her designer clothing.

The situation is now under control as backup police arrest the robbers and provide new clothing for the shit-stained officers.

"Haven't had a Code Brown called in in some time," jokes one backup officer.

"I think you mean a 'Code Dwayne,'" jokes the other backup officer.

Shelby is still on the floor, half in shock, half in relief. It's been an intense 10 minutes. Dwayne turns to his girl.

"I'll clean that ass up, baby. You're my girl."

"Oh, Dwayne, I love you. Can you believe eight people just shit themselves in the last five minutes?"

A once again confident Dwayne St. Thomas smiles.

"Shit happens, babe. Shit happens." Dwayne looks around at the totally disgusting scene and chuckles. Hildy and Montana are helping each other up.

"I'll be damned, Glancer Dark, you forgot to mention that, Conrad," he says to himself, finally understanding how his powers work.

Dwayne flips the switch to the Gasmart Station, so it says "closed" as he and Shelby walk out to the Chevy Spark.

"Hang tight, babe. I got some plastic tarp in the trunk. Don't want to ruin the leather in this baby."

Dwayne pops the trunk and gets out a bag. He starts emptying it out. First, a towel. Second, a few water bottles and some colognes. And finally, a pair of boxer shorts and some scrub pants.

"What in the world is that, Dwayne?"

"This, Shelby, is what I call the 'Shit Kit.' Never leave home without it. I came up with the idea a couple days back when I sharted outside the diner, and look, just days later, it came in handy."

"How does it work?"

"Well, Shelby, when someone defecates themselves as you have here today, they go to their Shit Kit. One towel to clean off the physical shit, then apply the water bottles to the affected area and wipe with the second towel. Next, you apply cologne to the affected region, and finally, you slip on some fresh briefs and pants, and you are good to go. Smooth sailing until you find a shower."

"Wow, Dwayne, you really are amazing."

Dwayne lights a smoke as he fills up the Spark gas tank.

"All in a day's work, Shelby. Now let's go see that movie."

Shelby, all fresh from the Shit Kit, opens the passenger door of the Spark for Dwayne.

"Get in, I'll drive. Guess we won't need the tarp now, will we, Dwayne?"

"Just leave it in there, babe. The night is young."

They drive off to the movie, a happier-than-ever couple.

CHAPTER 10
CONNECTING THE DOTS

It's just two days before White Pants Festival. Dwayne and Larry are at the bowling alley pounding some Glancer Darks. Dwayne is on cloud nine. He has discovered the secrets to how his powers work: Glancer Dark.

"Are you excited about the White Pants Festival, Larry? I know I sure am."

"Honestly, Dwayne, I don't know what you're up to. First, this stupid superpower of making people shit their pants that YOU DON'T HAVE. And secondly, White Pants Festival? Really? We despise that night. The bars always end up too packed and sucking. Why are you so obsessed with going?"

Larry does not yet know of the robbery at the Gasmart Station and the undeniable emergence of Dwayne's powers. Dwayne has decided to not try to convince anyone he has power. Perhaps it would be better if he knew. The more he uses it, he figures, the more they will all learn on their own.

"Larry, you will know when it's all over. At the end of the night, you will know!"

"You're scaring me, Dwayne. You sound like Apollo Creed right before the Russian killed him in 'Rocky 4'. Maybe I'll just skip it and hang out at the bar. Sounds like it may be bad news. Then again, I heard Dirty Urine is headlining. I love their song, 'Urination Not a Country.' Nah, still, I don't think so."

"That's nonsense, Larry. You and Marie are already committed to going. Come on, man, we always do the same thing: hang out at the Landing Strip, maybe bowl, and go to the Tainted Horse. Let's branch out. Let's wear white pants and black t-shirts and hang out with the privileged people."

A waitress comes up to Dwayne and Larry.

"Can I get you guys another round?"

"Another bucket of Glancer Dark," replies Dwayne.

"Sorry, we are all out of Glancer Dark. How about the regular Glancer?"

A pissed-off Dwayne stares at the waitress until she shits herself.

"Oh my god, I am so sorry, I thought it was a small fart," as she runs off, shit dripping out of her skirt every step of the way.

Larry stares at Dwayne. Dwayne smiles.

"No!"

"Yes!" replies Dwayne.

"You really can make people crap their pants?"

Dwayne has now confirmed what Larry thought was impossible.

"The other day, I figured it out when the Gasmart Station was getting jacked. It has to be Glancer Dark, Larry. When I told you my powers failed me at the restaurant, I drank regular Glancer. That's what happened."

Larry looks at Dwayne in amazement. He has never been around anyone with superpowers, let alone been best friends with anyone who possessed one.

Larry and Dwayne continue to bowl in silence for several minutes. Another waitress brings them a bucket of Glancers. Dwayne shakes his head but decides not to abuse his power.

"I know you boys wanted Glancer Dark, but it has sold more than we expected. The entire city is almost out. Gonna be a few weeks before they can get production to meet demands. This beer is really taking off. Enjoy the regular Glancers."

Dwayne has a look of panic in his eyes. Will he be able to secure enough Glancer Dark to pull off White Pants Festival?

"Shit, I need to go to the Gasmart Station. I forgot to buy beer."

"Sounds like a common mistake Dwayne. This is unbelievable. What kind of sick power is that, and how did you get it."

"I told you. Conrad Glancer came to me in a dream."

"I don't know what to say about that, Dwayne. I mean, on the one hand, I think you are crazy and full of shit, no pun intended. On the other hand, I have now witnessed two people crap themselves in front of you, and I have heard about several others. I mean, tell me, Dwayne, what is the end game? What are you possibly hoping to accomplish with this power other than to embarrass poor girls like that waitress? She did nothing to you. It's kind of messed up, Dwayne."

Dwayne looks somber.

"I admit that may have been an abuse of my powers. I was wrong to make that waitress shit her pants. She was a nice girl and did not deserve that. But, connect the dots, Larry. The power doesn't last forever, according to Conrad."

"Oh, yes, I forgot, Conrad Glancer is behind all of this. The ghost of Conrad Glancer, I should specify. And connect the dots, Dwayne. What is that supposed to mean?"

Hildy and Montana have now entered the bowling alley and spot Dwayne and Larry. They walk up, each holding a bowling ball. Hildy's ball has "Montana" engraved in it.

"Do the two of you follow me?" asks Dwayne.

"I have to hand it to you, Dwayne. That was one hell of a robbery the other day. Did you see all the poo?"

"Piss off, Montana."

Hildy chimes in. "I don't know what happened in that Gasmart Station, Dwayne, but it seems like shit follows you everywhere. Don't tell Montana to piss off. He's my man. He belongs to the MacMuphyn. I told you the other day, and I will tell you again, you are to treat Montana with respect."

Larry interjects, "We challenge the two of you to a bowl-off. You two versus the Stain and me. The top combined score wins. The loser has to pay the bar tab for the other party."

"Not to worry. I have Hildy's credit card. Challenge accepted."

"No, no, no! I'm not bowling with these assholes. Dwayne St. Thomas, I will see you in hell," yells Hildy.

"Hell is in two days, Hildy, and you sure as shit will see me," replies Dwayne

"Two days," she asks.

"That's right, the festival."

Hildy is not amused.

"White Pants Festival?"

"That's right, babe."

Montana chimes in

"Did you know—"

Hildy interrupts, "Shut up, Montana. What are you doing at White Pants Festival, Stain?" They won't let your kind in. Don't you dare attend my favorite night of the year."

Larry has not connected the dots—yet.

"Oh, my god," he says

"What? What, Larry?" pleads Hildy.

"I'm connecting the dots."

"I'm confused," adds Montana with a look of bewilderment on his face.

Dwayne, Hildy and Larry yell at Montana to shut up.

Dwayne stares at Montana, and he shits himself

"Ugh, another shart, Hildy. Did you know that the chili you made doesn't agree with me? Damn, this is the third pair of short pants I ruined this week."

Montana runs to the bathroom leaving Hildy, Dwayne and Larry at the bowling lane.

Hildy yells at Montana as he walks away.

"You're gross, Montana. Even Dwayne only did this once to me."

She turns her attention back to Dwayne and Larry. "Pretty soon he is going to have no short pants left to wear. What the hell is going on in this town? Everybody is shitting all over the place in public. Tread lightly St. Thomas. As for you Larry, you mopped up my shit once, I can sure make it happen again. Stay away from White Pants Festival, both of you!"

She walks off to follow Montana to the bathroom. Larry takes a long look at Dwayne.

"Is it true, Dwayne?"

"Yes, Larry. White Pants Festival will see Dwayne St. Thomas complete his revenge on all the people who have done him wrong throughout these years."

Dwayne lights a Doral and chugs a Glancer. Larry has a big grin on his face.

"You are a bad man Dwayne St. Thomas. A bad, bad man."

They both laugh out loud.

As the two of them wrap up their bowling match, Dwayne notices the television running a story on Glancer. The volume is not on, and they are unsure what is happening.

"Looks pretty serious," says Larry.

"How can we find out what is going on?"

"Easy, Dwayne, I have the Information Super Highway on my portable. I will look it up."

Larry breaks out his cell phone and begins to look up Glancerville News.

"Damn, Dwayne, that waitress wasn't kidding. Not only is there a shortage of Glancer Darks, but people are also blaming it for the recent defecations around the city. Seems like all public defecations of the last week have a common theme: Glancer Dark bottles all around the crime scene."

"Shit!" exclaims Dwayne.

CHAPTER 11

ALWAYS THE ANSWER

It is one day before the White Pants Festival, and Dwayne St. Thomas has a lot on his mind. He needs to make sure he secures enough Glancer Dark to pull off his revenge. But first things first: he wants to keep his follow-up appointment with Dr. Gross. Dwayne is interested to see if the doctor has any advice for him moving forward.

The receptionist welcomes Dwayne with her usual giggles. This time, however, there is no waiting. Dwayne walks right into the office and has a seat on the sofa.

"Dwayne," begins Dr. Gross, "after hearing your story, I really need to know about your childhood. I think you need to draw from the past to move forward. Do you have a

plan to get past this other than drinking Glancers all day?"

"I have a plan," assured Dwayne as he lights a smoke. "I think that in 48 hours, I will be a lot further past this than I have in the last 20 years.

"As for my childhood," he continues, "it was just like any other kid's childhood. My parents were good folks, hard workers. I hung out around the neighborhood and was a pretty accepted kid. All I wanted to do was have a few friends and enjoy life. All of that changed after the incident."

"You mean when you shit your pants on Hildy MacMuphyn at the sophomore dance."

An annoyed Dwayne confirms.

"Rick Townsend, that asshole, he will pay a dear price tomorrow night."

Dr. Gross seems concerned. "Tell me a little about tomorrow night, Dwayne."

"Can't, Doc."

"Dwayne, you mentioned to me last week that your relationship with your family is all but over since you ruined their lives. Is it important to you to re-establish that bond, and have you made an effort to do so? I think it would go a long way towards your healing."

"My family dropped me like a cheap prom dress the second things got tough for me around Glancerville. They cared more about their reputation than their bullied son."

"It must be hard, Dwayne, all of the bullying, and on top of that, your older brother Dwight having his way with Marie through his college years."

"He did not," Dwayne retorted. "Marie would never sleep with a scumbag like Dwight."

"Of course not, Dwayne. Forget I said anything. Moving on, I think I know what may help you."

"I'm ready for it. Lay it on me, Doc."

"Dwayne, I want you to write a letter to your mother, father, and Dwight, explaining to them how abandoning you has affected your life. On top of that, I want you to apologize for ruining their reputation and ask for forgiveness. Also, cut back a bit on the Glancers. I think the booze may be affecting your judgment."

Dwayne looks at the doctor in frustration.

"I can't believe you charge $100 an hour for advice like that, Doc. Quit drinking Glancer? Are you nuts? Maybe you should be the one on the sofa of shame. I appreciate your services, but I think I have a new doctor moving forward, his name is Dr. Conrad Glancer."

Dwayne stands up from the sofa, lights another smoke, and points his finger directly at Dr. Nelson Gross.

"I'll tell you another thing, Son of Nel. Hell is about to freeze over, and I'm the ice."

Dr. Gross looked startled.

"I'll have my parents send your final payment via the electronic transfer of money, otherwise known as The Venmo! Have a good life, Doc!"

Dwayne exits the doctor's office and walks to the Spark. He stops and takes a long hard stare at his beloved ride.

"Come on, Sparky. Let's go find some Glancer Dark and get ready for tomorrow."

Dwayne searches all over Glancerville East for Glancer Dark but is having a tough time finding even a bottle. It seems as if the news report is accurate. It *is* in high demand.

The Gasmart Station is temporarily closed from the robbery, so he doesn't know where to go. Finally, at long last, he walks into a drug store on the seediest strip of the East and spots Glancer Dark. He picks up a case and loads it in the Spark.

"Crisis avoided."

Dwayne drives back to the Lost Souls Lofts, parks the car, and sits on the hood of his car. Over the next several hours, he drinks several Glancer Darks. He is nervous yet excited about the next day's events. He doesn't know exactly how it will play out, but he knows it will be memorable. His mind is racing with questions. How should he use his powers? What is the best strategy? He's on unfamiliar turf at White Pants Festival.

Tipsy, Dwayne decides to head into his apartment rather than trek to the Landing Strip. On his way there, he runs into Larry, who is just getting home from work. Larry installs cable at the local cable company.

"Hey there, Lare-Bear. How about a cold Glancer Dark?"

Dwayne hands Larry a beer, and they sit on the hood of Larry's car and talk quickly turns to the next evening.

"Be careful, DST. Don't mess around tomorrow night. These people at White Pants Festival have money and could make your life miserable."

Larry thinks about what he just said and begins laughing.

"Ha, make your life miserable. What was I thinking? It can't get much worse than it is now. Fire away Stain."

Larry and Dwayne drink the remaining beers in the parking lot while continuing their conversation.

"Shit, Dwayne. We finished off all the Glancer Darks, and there's a shortage. What are you going to do tomorrow? Wasn't that your supply?"

Dwayne lights up a Doral.

"At ease, Lare-Bear. The drug store two miles away had several cases. I'll go there first thing in the morning and pick up another few. Let's go wrap our teeth around a few beers at the Landing Strip."

Larry and Dwayne call an Uber and head off to the Landing Strip. They stay there until 2 a.m. and cap off the night with a few cold ones at the Tainted Horse. Dwayne decides no matter what, he's not using his powers the night before White Pants Festival. He wants to be at his strongest the next day. After a few cold beers, Larry and Dwayne stumble back to their apartment complex. Dwayne, of course, has his final two beers on the couch before bedding down. He finally falls asleep close to 4 a.m.

Eight hours later, Dwayne awakens to the most anticipated day in his life.

This is not just any day. It is September 25, the day Dwayne has been waiting for ever since Conrad Glancer bestowed his powers onto him. Dwayne finally crawls out of bed around 12:30 to see the news broadcast with the usual anchors, Greg and Jane. He finishes a half-full beer on his nightstand as the broadcasters discuss the highly anticipated event taking place that night.

"Well, Jane, it looks like White Pants Festival is upon us tonight, and as previously reported, city officials expect record crowds in the downtown area."

"Yeah, Greg, almost every big name in Glancerville is expected to attend. City officials say if you want to go out and have a few drinks but not be part of the scene, good luck. Might be a good night to stay at home."

"Sounds wild, Jane. I wish I could just stay at home and just walk my dog."

"I bet, Greg. I just hope you meant your canine," laughs Jane.

"Actually, no such luck," she continues. "Both Greg and I will be live at White Pants Festival tonight, hosting the live feed."

"In other news," begins Greg, "Glancer Dark beer has been recalled and is no longer available in stores or bars. As previously speculated, the beer has been found at the scene of the crime of many of the city's recent public defecations. People were so concerned that Conrad Glancer III ordered the recall. He was not forced into it. All Glancer Dark was removed from shelves no later than midnight last night. Looks like when it comes to dark beer, Glancer is not always the answer. Glancer had this to say when asked about the situation."

Conrad Glancer III appears on screen:

"It's a small hiccup. They can't blame this surge of people crapping their pants on us, but we will check out our ingredients. If removing Glancer Dark from the shelves for a couple weeks makes people keep their undies clean, well, we will do so. My grandfather's dream was for Glancer Dark to make a splash. We just want to make sure it's the right splash. We plan to restock the shelves once our investigation is complete. Long live Glancer and Glancer Dark! No matter what flavor, Glancer is always the answer!"

Greg chimes in, "I have never heard of a beer company blamed for an outcry of public defecation. Conrad Glancer III is fighting the good fight."

"It's a crappy situation Greg, any way you look at it."

Dwayne, still lounging in bed, is outraged. It seems like he moves one step forward and takes two steps back. He looks at the newspaper and the front page is dedicated to White Pants Festival. There is no way his dream of getting revenge on Rick and all the people that did him wrong will go to waste. He knows he needs to figure something out. He is furious at himself for drinking the whole case of Glancer Dark in the parking lot with Larry the night prior before going out to the Landing Strip for beers. His backup plan of going to the drug store for additional cases is now out the window as the news reports there are none available after midnight the night before.

"This has got to be a joke. I'm totally screwed, I finally learned how to use my powers, and they run out of Glancer Dark. Not on my watch."

Dwayne started shopping. Surely someone did not get the memo and has a case or two of Glancer Dark on hand. No such luck. Store after store, block after block, Glancer Dark is nowhere to be found.

Dwayne returns home to contemplate the situation. He is in deep thought as he looks around his apartment. He again stares at the ad for White Pants Festival. Without Glancer Dark, he'll have no power, and with no power, what good is White Pants Festival?

"I really screwed the pooch this time. How could I have been so foolish?"

Just then, the phone rings. Dwayne answers it and at the other end of the line is Shelby.

"Hey, boo. I was in the neighborhood and thought I would swing by. I have a gift for you."

Dwayne is in no mood for visitors.

"Shelby, if this is that harness you always talk about, today is not the best day."

"Dwayne, get your mind out of the gutter. I'll be pulling up in the parking lot in a few minutes. Meet me outside, please."

Dwayne walks outside and sees Shelby pull up in her Smart Car. She can sense Dwayne is not in a good space.

"What's with you? You seem agitated."

"Just stressing out with it being the anniversary and all. It's been a tough 20 years."

Dwayne does not want to reveal the truth about what is happening. His powers, the Glancer Dark, and lack thereof. He doesn't want Shelby to know about his gift. Like most people with superpowers, he doesn't want to be loved for all the wrong reasons. It's the burden Dwayne now carries.

"Ok, Dwayne, I understand, but before I leave, I have something in my trunk for you."

"Hey, this day is turning around," smiles Dwayne.

"Not that trunk, smart ass. The trunk of the Smart Car."

Dwayne and Shelby walk to the back of the car, and Shelby opens up the trunk. There lies the greatest sight ever imaginable to Dwayne. Five cases of Glancer Dark. He's in disbelief.

"They recalled it, so I figured I would sneak it out the back and give it to you. I know you always said you would rather see a house burn down than a beer go to waste."

Dwayne lights a cigarette and looks at Shelby.

"Shelby, you have made me the happiest man in the world. You really have no idea how much this means to me. A couple more episodes like this, and you may get the vacation to Detroit you have always wanted."

"DST, you are my man. I just want to be your forever, Shelby. I am your oil. You are my gas."

Dwayne puts his arms around Shelby and gives her a big hug.

"I am always going to be your gas, Shelby."

Dwayne looks at his watch. He knows it is time to secure the Glancer Dark. He unloads them from her car and moves them into his fridge.

"Better get this stuff off the streets before the cops catch wind."

CHAPTER 12

DON'T FLUSH ME AWAY

Dwayne has secured his Glancer Dark beer thanks to Shelby, and it is now 4 p.m. The day of the White Pants Festival, and he could not be more excited. He turns on the television set to see the latest update on the festival. The live feed has already begun, although the event is not expected to open to the public for a few hours. Many onlookers are tailgating outside the designated area in anticipation.

"Well, it looks like White Pants Festival is finally upon us, and downtown is getting ready for a wild night. We went to the streets to interview some folks doing a bit of tailgating as they awaited the evening festivities. We spoke with this young lady just moments ago," Greg says.

Hildy appears on the television screen.

"Hello, Greg, so excited to be on screen with you. You are so hot. Anyhow, this is so exciting. I mean, it is truly the night of the year when the accomplished, wealthy, hardworking Glancerville residents get to dress up and enjoy themselves. All the great people are here. I am looking forward to mingling with the crowd and drinking some Old Fashions and white wine. I will probably be an absolute disaster at the bar later, but that's everyone else's problem. And Dirty Urine is playing. I am so excited! I hope they open with 'Don't Flush Me Away.' I love that song, especially the acoustic version!"

"I hate that woman," mumbles Dwayne.

The camera swings back to the news anchors.

"I bet you loved running into girls like that at the bar after White Pants Festival in your heyday, Greg?"

"True, Jane. One of my favorite nights of the year as a lad. I always knew I was a great 'anchor.' We will see you all tonight at the most anticipated event of September, White Pants Festival."

Dwayne begins pacing back and forth throughout his apartment, thinking about how the night will play out. He is going to the festival with Larry and Marie as planned. He feels guilty for not insisting Shelby attend, but she stood her ground against it, and Dwayne respects that. He calls Larry and Marie to firm up plans. They are meeting at the Landing Strip at 5 p.m. for some pre-gaming festivities and then heading to the big event around 7.

The clock strikes 4:30.

Dwayne thinks back to the days of returning to school after he shit his pants all those years ago. Most of the kids just pointed and laughed. Rick was the one that took it the farthest. One time at the school talent show, Rick was doing standup comedy. Dwayne remembers his act vividly. Rick took the microphone and immediately began bullying Dwayne in his routine.

xxx

"Did you all hear that Elton John wrote the second version of 'Candle in the Wind' in memory of Princess Di? It's called 'Goodbye England's Rose.' It's really good. As a matter of fact, it has had so much success on the charts that he has announced there will be a third version of the song coming out in a couple weeks. This one is dedicated to our very own Dwayne St. Thomas. Do you know what it is called?"

The crowd looks in anticipation.

"It's called 'Candle that Shits its Pants in the Wind.'"

The entire gymnasium erupts in laughter. Poor Dwayne just puts his head down as usual. Only Larry was there for him. He put his arm around Dwayne.

"Don't let it bother you, little buddy. You are still my best friend."

xxx

Dwayne also remembers the challenges he had getting jobs and finding dates. He eventually resorted to the seedy strip clubs just for female companionship. To cope, he began smoking three packs a day and drinking Glancer after Glancer. Friends were concerned about Dwayne's growing bad habits and declining health. Who could blame him, though? He was shot down before he even entered his prime. He had no family, no wife, and no confidence. He was a janitor in the very school where the incident occurred. He could not even escape it at the workplace. Even students less than half his age were giving him a hard time.

4:45 p.m. rolls along, and there is a knock on the door. Dwayne opens the door to see Larry standing there.

"Hey, Stain, ready for the big evening? I was going to meet you at the Strip, but I got out of work early, so I figured I would stop by. Are you ready to rock and roll tonight, DST?"

Dwayne has an evil grin on his face, and he lights up a Doral.

"Does a Glancer taste great? Yes, Larry, you have no idea what this means! Tonight, my mission will be completed after all!"

"I'm dying of curiosity."

Dwayne walks to the kitchen and returns, holding two cases of Glancer Dark.

"Help me carry these to the Spark, Larry. They are coming with us tonight."

"Holy hell, Stain, this stuff is outlawed! You're not playin' around. This is our weapon of choice, I see."

"You don't bring a knife to a gunfight, Lare-Bear. You bring Glancer Dark."

Dwayne begins to look for a screwdriver and finally finds one.

"Come on, Larry, shotgun a Glancer Dark with me before we go."

"Wow, you mean business."

Larry agrees, and they proceed to shotgun two beers each.

"That tasted amazing, Dwayne. Let's go do this."

Larry and Dwayne go down to the Spark and load the Glancer Dark. Dwayne starts the ignition and revs the engine a few times. They're on their way. They arrive at the Landing Strip a few minutes later and walk inside to meet Marie. The night has begun, and White Pants Festival is upon them.

The mood is electric in the Landing Strip. White pants are everywhere as folks are tailgating for the big night.

"I am so excited!" cries Marie as she sees Dwayne and Larry.

She is wearing tight leather white pants and a very revealing black blouse.

The friends hang out for a few hours, enjoying drinks and sharing memories. Dwayne is going back and forth to the Spark every few minutes to pound a Glancer Dark to ensure he is well above his six-beer quota. The clock strikes 7, and Marie suggests they leave for the event. Larry steps in.

"Before we go to White Pants Festival, I want to propose a toast to my best friend, Dwayne St. Thomas."

"Oh Larry, that's so sweet!" yells Marie.

Larry orders three Glancers and asks his friends to raise their beer.

He begins, "Dwayne, I have known you for 30 years, and you are my best friend. Your life has been a living hell for the last 20 ever since you shit all over Hildy MacMuphyn at the sophomore dance. I even thought of canceling my friendship with you, Dwayne, because being your friend was a liability. Girls would not talk to me either, and I was immediately considered a loser. You basically ruined most of my last 20 years, Dwayne. With all that said, let's have fun tonight, and whatever you have planned for White Pants Festival, may it be amazing."

"Aw, Larry, that was so heart-felt," says Marie.

Dwayne gives Larry a hug.

"Thanks, man. I'll make it all up to you, Lare-Bear. When I complete my mission, you will reap the benefits of being Dwayne St. Thomas' best friend."

"Well, should we call an Uber," asks Marie.

Dwayne lights a smoke and takes the last sip of his beer.

"We can surely Uber, but keep in mind Marie, tonight, Dwayne St. Thomas is behind the wheel of Glancerville at long last. Tonight will be my finest hour. Tonight, we will see, never to be doubted again, that Glancer really is the answer."

The three get in the Uber and drive off to White Pants Festival.

CHAPTER 13
I AM DWAYNE ST. THOMAS

The sheer excitement is almost too much to contain as Dwayne and his friends exit the Uber just blocks away from the festival. It is a gorgeous evening and the festival is under way when they arrive.

The streets are packed with middle-aged men and women wearing white pants and black shirts, parading from bar to bar.

Main Street is where all the action takes place. It has high-scale restaurants, several art galleries and some popular bars. It is the commercial mecca of Glancerville. Their first stop is the ritzy Black Bear Bar. This is a classy joint, a place that does not even sell Glancer beer.

Dwayne has managed to sneak a few Glancer Darks into the establishment thanks to Marie's purse and the man purse he slung over one shoulder. He moves through the crowd and makes his way to the bar's balcony. He is wearing a black t-shirt that reads "White Pants Festival" in white lettering and some white painter pants. He is overcome with anxiety and anticipation all at the same time.

"Have you ever seen so many people in white pants?" asks Dwayne. "It's amazing."

"Actually, I have, Dwayne. I was at White Pants Festival two years ago," says Marie sarcastically.

She then takes the beer out of Dwayne's hands and sets it on the nearby table. She looks Dwayne square in the eye.

"Dwayne, there are a lot of innocent people out there. It's not too late to call this off, whatever the hell you have planned."

"Yeah, Stain, I don't know what you think you are going to do, but a lot of innocent people could get hurt," adds Larry.

Dwayne turns to his concerned friends and says with a smirk.

"Nothing a little Downy or Tide couldn't clean up?"

Dwayne continues, "Save it for a rainy day, Larry. My time has come. And to be honest, I have nothing planned, only moving visuals in my head. Like all great artists, I wait to see what colors land on the canvas we call life. Now I must hit the streets and show everyone that Dwayne St. Thomas is nothing to be fooled with."

Larry and Marie know they are fighting a losing battle. Nothing would keep Dwayne from fulfilling the prophecy played out to him by Conrad Glancer himself several days earlier. Dwayne takes another beer from his man bag and chugs it down. He puts two in his pocket and begins to walk off. Just then, his portable rings. It's Shelby calling. Although he does not want to, Dwayne answers the phone.

"Hey babe, coming to see my work of art tonight?"

There is a pause on the other end of the line.

"What do you mean, Dwayne? I was calling you to tell you to be careful. The police are after that Montana kid.

Apparently, he robbed an ex-girlfriend's house, and his cover was blown. You were right. He is a fraud and wanted in many cities for years. They believe he will try to hide in the crowd tonight at White Pants Festival and then escape town by stealing someone's purse using their cash and cards for his getaway. Probably Hildy's. Dwayne, be careful."

Dwayne thinks for a second.

"Does Hildy know?"

"I don't think so, Dwayne. She may be his victim tonight. I think they are going to White Pants Festival together."

Dwayne thinks for a moment. If the cops were after him, would he go to the most popular event of the year, hoping to not get caught? No, but Montana sure as hell would.

"Okay, babe, I'll be looking out for Montana."

Dwayne does not give another thought to Montana after he hangs up the phone as he walks down Main Street. As he strolls, he sees the main podium. Mayor Sandy Wilson begins to address the crowd.

Mayor Wilson is in his second term, and White Pants Festival, thanks to Rick Townsend, has really helped the economic revival of Glancerville. It's helped Mayor Wilson's profile, too. Outside of Glancer Distribution, White Pants Festival's revenue is one of the biggest sources of money for the city.

"Welcome one and all to the 10th annual White Pants Festival! There is no more special time of year in Glancerville than tonight. Our town is known for many things. Good people, Glancer beer, our very own rock 'n roll band, Dirty Urine, the kid that shit himself at the sophomore dance 20 years ago when he shat all over Hildy MacMuphyn, and most importantly, White Pants Festival. Enjoy the music, the food, the art, and the drinks. Please be mindful of the others when you show up at the bars trashed. And ladies, nobody is fooled when three of you enter the single-stall restroom together. Remember, cocaine is still illegal. Let's all be mindful adults.

"I'd like to thank past legends of Glancerville who cannot attend tonight, most notably Dwight St. Thomas," he continues. "Certainly, this was one night of the year when that young legend threw his manhood around like a lasso. Godspeed to you wherever you are, Dwight. And last but not least, this night would not be possible without the vision and hard work of Rick Townsend. Rick, I salute you, and so does all of Glancerville. You keep giving back, and you are a model for our young people."

Dwayne shakes his head as he continues down the street. He spots his main target, the man of the hour himself, Rick, who is next up on the big stage following the mayor's comments. Rick is being interviewed by the news station and is wearing his usual white leather pants, black socks, and white loafers. He has a black t-shirt that is two sizes too small and a pair of vintage black sunglasses. His hair is more slicked back than usual. The news reporters are eating up everything Rick has to say.

"Basically, I consider White Pants Festival my baby. My ex, Hildy, and I were always brainstorming on how we could get all the well-to-do people of the city out on the same evening in the same gathering."

"Textbook Rick," thinks Dwayne.

"After Hildy got shit on at the sophomore dance, I vowed I would never subject her to such a low-class event. I thought and thought and eventually came up with White Pants Festival. As for Hildy and me, we are broken up. She belongs to the streets now."

Jane interrupts, "Excuse my Mr. Townsend, you mentioned your ex was the one who got shit on at the sophomore dance. Was that the Dwayne St. Thomas incident?"

"Well, I wasn't going to say his name, but yeah, that's his name. He lives in Glancerville East in the Lost Souls Lofts and hangs out at the Landing Strip Bar. Anyway, after that incident, I was like, man, something like that can't happen at my White Pants Festival. When you're here, you'd better hold onto your load."

Greg and Jane laugh hysterically.

Rick looks away from the interview and spots Dwayne smoking and drinking a beer.

Rick wastes no time as he points out Dwayne.

"Speak of the devil, that's Dwayne right there. Nobody likes a rat Greg, but I believe he is carrying a banned substance. He's got a Glancer Dark."

The news anchors look over at Dwayne. The two of them always reference his incident of 20 years ago. And now, here he is, live in the flesh! At that moment, Greg walks toward Dwayne.

Dwayne is trembling in his shoes. He is not sure about what is about to happen, only that the wheels are already in motion. He thought he would be in control of the night's events, but now it seems as if the events are governing him.

Greg steps right next to Dwayne, and with the microphone on and camera rolling, he speaks to him.

"Mr. St. Thomas, would you mind if we did an interview with you? You are a legend in this town, yet nobody has ever heard your story. Is it now time we hear the other side of what happened 20 years ago tonight? Would you mind answering a few questions?"

Rick is staring, just feet away. "Yeah, Dwayne, this is your moment to shine. Tell them your story. Get it off your chest once and for all. Fly, Free Bird."

Dwayne is startled. He has obviously never been interviewed for anything, and now, on the biggest night of the year at the biggest festival in Glancerville, they want to put him on the air. He takes a sip of his beer and tries to get his anxiety under control. At first, he thinks about enacting his powers right then and there, but for some reason, he is scared. He has cold feet. Something has come over him. Is the moment too big?

Dwayne exhales the final puff of his smoke in Greg's direction.

"I don't think so, sorry," replies Dwayne as he slowly walks away.

20 years have passed. Dwayne's life has been a wild ride—a mess at that. Booze, cigarettes, cheap women, and then there were the bad things. Depression, fear of going out in public, not finding love, and leaving a legacy behind that nobody would really want. It all came down to tonight and

the new power he had been given. Why be interviewed and laughed at all over the city when the nightly news airs? Tonight was supposed to be about Dwayne's revenge.

At that moment, Larry catches up with him. He's out of breath, obviously concerned.

"Geez, Dwayne, thanks for walking off. Marie and I have been looking all over for you. I heard they wanted to interview you after Rick pointed you out. Probably a good idea that you said no. You don't want the entire festival staring at you."

Dwayne gives Larry a confused look.

"It wouldn't have been on the news until later tonight or in the morning, Larry. No one here would see me. I am just camera shy and don't want video footage of me, that's all."

"No, look," says Marie. She points 50 yards ahead. There's a screen big enough to fit inside of a movie theater. It's showing the news channel's live feed from the festival. On the screen is Rick, hamming it up with Greg and Jane..

"They are running that shit live, Stain. It's a live feed. Whoever is interviewed is live to the entire crowd."

Dwayne stops for a second. "You mean to tell me that when someone is on camera here tonight, they are staring at the entire crowd, and the entire crowd is staring back?" he asks.

Larry and Marie begin to explain to Dwayne the concept of how a live feed works. They pull up videos on You-Tube and Google until he eventually understands the concept.

"Rick was the first to be on the live stream. It's all live now, DST," said Larry.

The endless interviewing of Rick Townsend continues. "So, I said to myself, Rick, you can do this. You can make White Pants Festival a reality. I was the best athlete and the most popular kid in Glancerville in High School. I T-boned more girls than anyone, except maybe Dwight St. Thomas. So, you know, why end it there? Why not take my total package into adulthood. So here we are, 10 years later, and this town is still eating out of my hand."

Thousands in the audience watch the live feed as they enjoy their cocktails and walk around the festival. They begin a loud chant: "Thank you, Rick. Thank you, Rick."

Rick is reveling in the attention. The tenth anniversary of the White Pants Festival has begun swimmingly. Dirty Urine takes the stage and begin tuning up their instruments.

Dwayne stops dead in his tracks as an idea occurs to him. This was like an idea like no other. An evil smirk spreads across his face. He fires up a Doral, cracks open a Glancer Dark, and begins to sip it. After a few drags, he crushes out the cigarette.

"Larry, Marie, I'll be back in a few minutes. It's time for me to make my move."

Marie and Larry look at Dwayne in confusion on this fateful night, but now they are about to find out what exactly it is.

"Shit, here we go," mumbles Larry.

Dwayne strides back over toward the news camera, where Rick is winding down his interview. He has an idea. If it works, shit is about to get real. The interview with Rick is finally over, and the band starts playing.

"Thank you so much for your precious time, Mr. Townsend, and good luck tonight and the next several years with the future of White Pants Festival."

"Sure has been nice visiting with you, as usual, Jane and Greg! Time for me to go kiss some babies and shake some hands," Rick chuckles as he spots Dwayne walking toward them. Rick looks at him a bit differently this time around. He has a semi-concerned look. Was Dwayne St. Thomas actually up to something tonight? And if so, could it be at his expense?

"Oh look, Baron Von Poo is coming back. You may get your interview after all," says Rick to Greg.

Rick and Dwayne lock eyes as Dwayne slowly moves forward toward the interview tent.

Just then, Dwayne grabs the microphone out of Rick's hand and looks at Jane and Greg.

"You wanted Dwayne St. Thomas. Well, now you have him. I'll do your interview."

Dwayne then turns toward Rick.

"I told you I would get revenge one day, Rick. That day has come."

Rick laughs at Dwayne.

"Whatever, Dwayne, do your thing. I have to be social."

He abruptly walks off as he points his finger at Dwayne.

"Don't test me, St. Thomas."

As Dwayne waits, Jane and Greg discuss what questions to ask him. He smokes another cigarette as he awaits his moment in the spotlight. Finally, after several minutes, they are ready to interview him.

The band stops playing as the crowd anxiously awaits the interview. Greg walks up to Dwayne and pulls him aside. At this point, the cameras are off, and no microphone is on.

"Dwayne, are you okay with this? The questions will be fair, I can promise you that. I think it would be good for you and all of Glancerville if we do this. What do you think?"

Dwayne looks away from Greg for a second and stares at Marie and Larry. Rick has not moved too far from the cameras. Curiosity has gotten the better of him. Montana and Hildy are now on the premises. It's all coming together. He finally knows what to do. He turns back to Greg.

"Go for it, Greg," says Dwayne as he cracks open another Glancer Dark. He is well beyond his required six beers for his powers to be fully effective. He is at least 13 deep.

The anchors are delighted. They have their man. They signal for the microphone and cameras to turn back on.

"Well, okay, let's get started," adds Jane.

The cameras begin rolling. Greg prepares to start the interview.

Dwayne St. Thomas is on the big screen on the big night.

Greg cautiously moves Dwayne into position as he is about to begin.

"Hello, ladies and gentlemen. We have a special guest joining us tonight for his first-ever interview. He is a legend here in Glancerville but maybe not for the reasons you think. Do you remember 20 years ago when someone pooped their pants while dancing with the prettiest girl at the sophomore dance? Well, we have that someone here with us right now who will enlighten his side of the story. That's right, folks! We are joined by none other than Dwayne St. Thomas!"

Once the name is said, there is a silence that comes across the entire White Pants Festival. People hush, and you could hear a pin drop within seconds. All eyes are turned to the gigantic screen showing the live feed.

Shelby, at the Gasmart Station, is watching it too. "Shit the bed, Dwayne, what have you gotten yourself into?"

Jane asks the first question. "Well, Dwayne, I will start. Can you confirm that it was actually you that committed the act 20 years ago? And what has life been like ever since?"

Dwayne pauses. He is still nervous, but he knows what he has to do.

"Well, Jane, it was me. I shit the hell out of my pants that night. I was dancing with a girl named Hildy, and it just happened. Turns out I had been tricked. Someone put eye drops in my Glancer beer. It was the first night that I was drinking Glancers, and I was doing good. I was four deep. My life since then has been a nightmare. I have been picked on and bullied, and I never have been able to live it down. But I am here tonight to face the city of Glancerville once and for all and say, 'Yes I am Dwayne St. Thomas, and I shit my

126

pants at the sophomore dance in 2001!' You can learn to deal with it, Glancerville. I am not hiding anymore. Except for a couple days ago, in a restaurant parking lot, I have not shit my pants since. To Hildy MacMuphyn, I am sorry you were the victim of my defecation. I can't listen to the song 'Free Bird' without feeling remorse. To my family, especially my brother, Dwight, I am sorry about your white short pants and ruining the good St. Thomas name."

Cheers emerge from the crowd. People are starting to like how Dwayne is coming out publicly to admit what happened. He is standing up to all bullies once and for all. Dwayne has always hidden, but not tonight. Dwayne is standing up for all the kids that had a bad situation happen but have never been able to put it behind them.

Greg asks, "Dwayne, you said you were a victim of someone putting eye drops in your beer. Did you ever find out who committed this vile act against you?"

This is his moment to make history, and Dwayne wastes no time.

"Yes, Greg, I sure do. The act was committed by Rick Townsend, the founder and COO of the White Pants Festival. He tricked me into having a fourth Glancer. I thought he was simply being my friend and trying to help me get the courage to ask Hildy to dance with me. He knew I always had a crush on her, and my chances of her dancing with me were low. I was a nobody, and it was football season. Hildy dated the offense, and it was going to be an uphill battle. But, thanks to Rick, I asked her to dance, only realizing several minutes later I fell right into his evil and grotesque trap."

The crowd goes crazy. Beer bottles are flying. It is anarchy. The White Pants Festival is a lie. Rick Townsend is not a good man, and Dwayne St. Thomas has exposed him for the fraud he really is.

Rick feels his cheeks grow warm. He panics. He never thought Dwayne would have the courage to actually expose him. He immediately becomes defensive.

"He's a liar, and it will be a cold day in hell before I ever admit to that. You messed with the wrong person, Baron Von Poo!" screams Rick.

It is utter chaos. The crowd is insane.

Marie runs up to the camera and hugs Dwayne. She grabs the microphone out of Jane's hands and begins speaking to the live feed.

"He's not lying. Rick owned up to it in my bar last week. It was Rick Townsend that drugged Dwayne with eye drops in his Glancer beer and made him shit all over Hildy."

As crowd chaos continues, Jane and Greg try to get the audience's attention so they can continue the interview. Rick flees. Things begin to calm down.

"Did you know that guy is running away?" Montana says to Hildy.

Hildy sternly turns to Montana.

"Go get him, Montana. Capture him. My life has been a lie. I can't believe it was Rick all along that was responsible for me getting shit on. Dwayne was just the supplier, and Rick was the denier. I mean, I always heard the rumors, but Rick said it was not true. No one on the first team would date me afterward. I was left dating the backup defense."

"As you wish, babe."

Montana chases after Rick. Meanwhile, Greg looks at Dwayne for a third question.

"Wow, Dwayne, what a night this has become! White Pants Festival will never be the same!"

Dwayne lights up another Doral, opens a Glancer Dark on camera, and replies, "No, Greg, it sure as shit won't! Do you mind giving me a close-up on the camera?'

Greg obliges, and the cameras close in on Dwayne.

At that point, Dwayne stares into the camera. He stares and stares until he starts getting the feeling. Thousands of eyes at the White Pants festival are staring right back at him on the camera. He is going for it in a way never imagined. Dwayne St. Thomas has figured out the best way to use his powers is via live broadcast feed.

"Gee, Dwayne, smoking on camera. We do not really allow that," Greg says.

Dwayne stares directly at Greg. He stares and stares. "Glancer is always the answer!" yells Dwayne at the top of his lungs.

"Oh, boy, Jane, please fly solo for a bit. I think I need to find the men's room," Greg says as he runs off with a huge brown stain on the back of his suit pants.

Dwayne looks back into the camera directly and stares.

All at once, the thousands and thousands of patrons of White Pants Night begin feeling their stomachs churning. One by one, hundreds by hundreds, they all start crapping their pants. Dwayne continues to stare as he pounds Glancer Dark after Glancer Dark on the air.

The camera continues to roll.

Greg and Jane have abandoned the post as Jane has shit her pants as well. The cameraman has left the camera idle on a tripod as he abandoned his post to crap himself. Montana, Hildy, Marie, Rick—they all shit their pants.

"Causality of war, sorry," says Dwayne as he winks at Marie and Larry.

The streets are a mess, and people are fleeing. The smell is god awful. Dwayne sees his work and admires it. He turns away from the camera, knowing his job is done. He has finally   gotten   his   revenge.

After admiring his work, Dwayne slowly walks towards his friends, all a mess of shit.

"I had a feeling this might happen. Come on, Marie and Larry. I have a change of clothes for you in the back of the Spark. Let's clean you up and wrap our teeth around a few beers at the Landing Strip."

Larry and Marie look at Dwayne.

"Looks like we will have to order an Uber Brown," jokes Larry.

Marie chimes in, "DST, your powers are no joke. You really did it. You brought down Rick Townsend and got your revenge."

"I never asked for glory, Marie, maybe just a glory hole. Let's go get some beers."

130

Laughing, Marie and Larry say, "Sure thing, Dwayne, let's go."

Across town, Montana tackles Rick and holds him to the ground. "Did you know I T-boned your girl, and now I am going to steal your wallet and credit cards and high tail it out of town? Give me all of your possessions."

Rick, knowing he is desperate, pleads for help.

"You'll never get away with it, Montana. We both have shit all over ourselves. Come with me. I have a safe getaway we can both hide out at."

.

"Getaway. What do you mean?"

Rick grabs Montana by his shitty shirt.

"Montana, you moron. Dwayne St. Thomas may have won tonight, but together, as a team, we can bring him down once and for all. He ruined my name and my festival tonight. Come with me, Montana. Let's escape tonight and plot our revenge on Dwayne St Thomas and rule Glancerville side by side. You're wanted by the cops. I am your only escape."

Montana, desperate himself, contemplates the proposal.

"That sound like a good idea?" he replies.

The men help each other up, duck down an alley, and into a safety zone near one of Rick's offices.

Safe at last in the alleyway at Rick's office, he and Montana have showered and are now in the hot tub trying to relax. The situation is awkward, but finally, Rick speaks up.

"I tell ya, Montana, I really don't like you, you mowed my lawn with Hildy, and frankly, I think you're a cocksucker; however, we have a common interest."

"Do tell," says Montana.

"We both have been wronged by Dwayne St. Thomas. He ruined my festival and made you shit your pants four times this week."

Montana pauses.

"Did you know I thought it was five times?"

Rick is not amused.

"Enough, Montana, I ruined Dwayne St. Thomas's life once, and I can do it again. Are you with me or not? I need to know now."

Montana smiles.

"I'm all in, Richard. I am all in."

CHAPTER 14

THE DARK GLANCER

Celebrations for Dwayne, Larry and Marie at the Landing strip ran late into the night. Dwayne returns home at 4 a.m. and sees Shelby waiting by his front door.

"Well, hey there Shelby girl, I didn't expect to see you."

Shelby has a gleam in her eye as she sees her boo.

"Dwayne, it was you that saved me the other night at the Gasmart Station during the robbery. Is it true? Can you make people shit their pants by staring at them?"

"Don't ever ask me about my powers Shelby," responds Dwayne. "Just know I will always protect you and anyone else I can."

"OK," she agrees.

The next morning, Dwayne wakes up with Shelby in his bed. The news is on as usual. The anchors are discussing record numbers for their morning broadcast following the previous evening events.

"Looks like the future of White Pants Festival is in jeopardy as Dwayne St. Thomas exposed COO Rick Townsend as a fraud. Geez Greg, Dwayne may be more of a legend in this town after last night than his brother Dwight."

"Let's not get out of hand here, Jane."

Dwayne lights a Doral as he and Shelby spoon.

"I just love a man who smokes in bed. So 1950s of you, Dwayne."

Dwayne blows a little puff her way.

"I'm a hungry Shelby. Let's go grab a bite to eat."

"Sure, boo. I'm glad it all worked out last night and you had your revenge on White Pants Festival. But what now?

"Shelby, my love, I only have six Glancer Darks left, and then I need to find a new road until the ban is lifted. The world is now my oyster, and my presence will be known."

Dwayne has a few Glancer Darks and hands Shelby the keys as they get in the Spark and head off to the restaurant. "I'm important now, Shelby, so no more drinking and driving for this guy." As Shelby drives, Dwayne smiles. He's on cloud nine.

They pull into the parking lot of the diner. As they enter, all heads turn in awe at the sight of Dwayne St. Thomas. Not everyone has realized his powers caused the mass shitting, but they all know he exposed Rick Townsend for being a fraud and he is a hero to many. Several patrons stand up and applaud.

"Thank you all, thank you, not necessary, but please, keep applauding, it's so nice, don't sit down," says Dwayne to the onlookers.

"Geez, Dwayne, you are really eating this up" says Shelby.

Dwayne secretly pours a couple Glancer Darks into a large 24-ounce cup from the diner, successfully finishing off his stash.

"Perhaps I will finish these beers and find one last victim," Dwayne says to Shelby.

Just then the waitress comes to the table and asks if they are ready to order their meal.

As usual, Dwayne takes the lead and orders for Shelby.

"We want two small cups of chili. How is it today? Spicy?" asks Dwayne.

"Baby, I'll be honest, it's a little bit runny," responds the waitress.

Dwayne looks at Shelby

"Better make those two large bowls then!"

They all laugh together.

How about something to drink?" she asks.

"I'm fine with this road beer I brought with me. The lady will have a coffee."

The waitress nods her head and walks away.

"Shelby, I'll be honest, I have almost finished these six Glancer Darks and nobody has been mean to me this entire day. I can't recall a day in the last 20 years this has happened. I don't think I am going to make anyone shit themselves today."

"Well, that's great Dwayne. It's only 11 a.m., but still, that is wonderful."

Dwayne looks deep in thought and then begins to speak.

"I don't know if and when my powers will ever be needed again. If never, so be it, but if so, I must answer the call."

Shelby is impressed by Dwayne's mature tone and looks deep into his eyes.

"Oh Dwayne, these last few weeks have been so memorable with you."

"Shelby, you better get a pen and paper, because I am something to write home about!"

Shelby looks at Dwayne, runs her fingers through his hair and says, "I do not know who you are right now, Dwayne, but I like it."

"Baby, you are not looking at Dwayne St. Thomas right now."

A confused Shelby asks, "Well then who am I looking at."

A smile spreads slowly over his face. "You can call me," he says with a dramatic pause, "the Dark Glancer."

THE END.

Made in USA - Kendallville, IN
80110_9781960620361
04.02.2023 1316